THE LYRIAN ALLIANCE

BOOK 2

THE LYRIAN ALLIANCE

BOOK 2

COLLEEN FORBES

THE SWAN WING

Cover Design: Damonza
Map Illustration: Hanna Sandvig
Formatting: Enchanted Ink Publishing

ISBN: 978-1-953568-03-8

Printed in the United States of America

TO AMBER

YOU DESERVE ALL THE DEDICATIONS THIS YEAR!

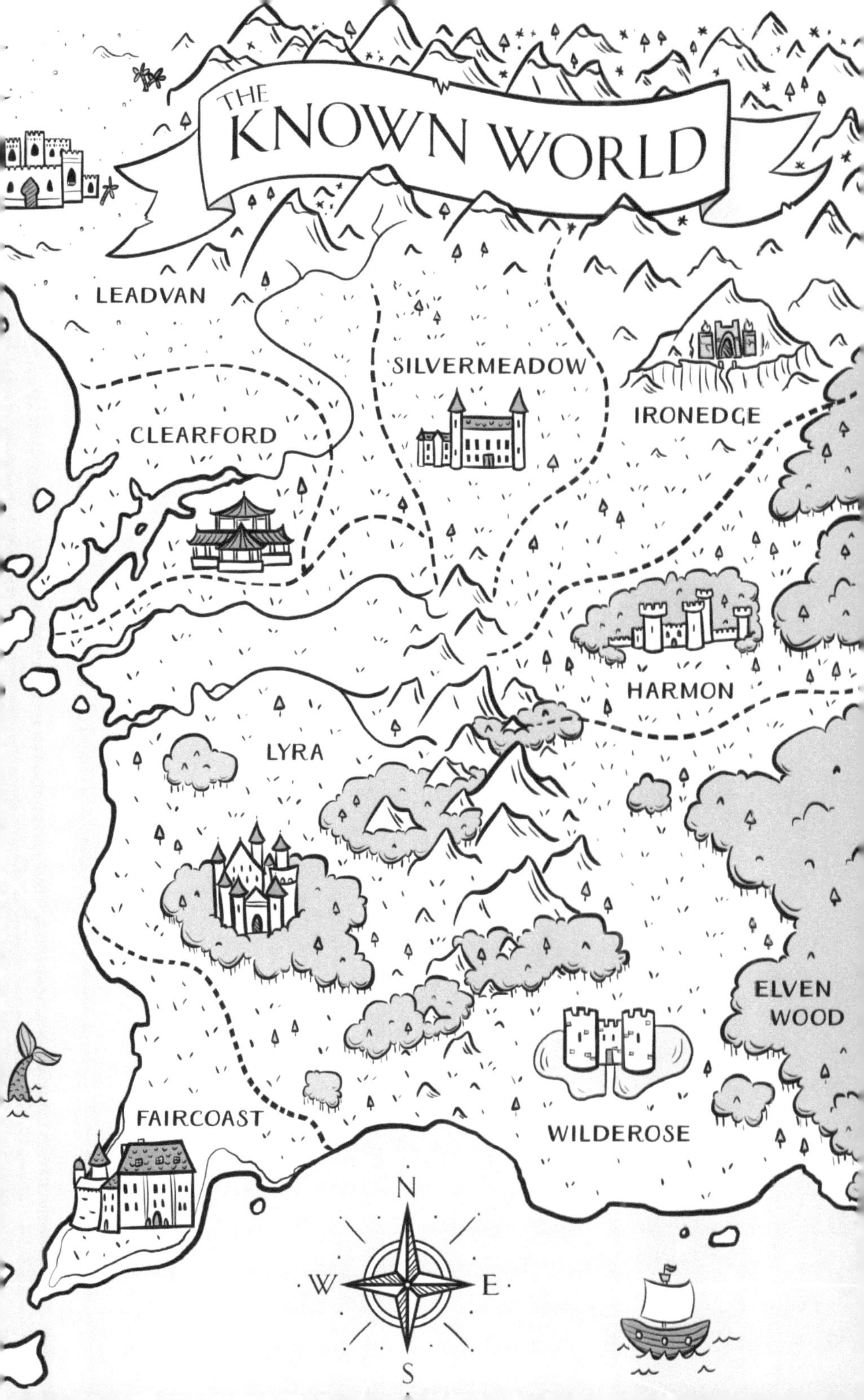
THE KNOWN WORLD
LEADVAN
SILVERMEADOW
CLEARFORD
IRONEDGE
HARMON
LYRA
ELVEN WOOD
FAIRCOAST
WILDEROSE
N
W
E
S

CHAPTER 1

Cress wished she had her knittind needles. They would have made a way better weapon than the embroidering need she had in her hand, if it came down to it.

Her heart hammered in her chest while the carriage jostled, the driver urging the horses to gallop away from the raiders attempting to attack them. The wheels bounced and ricocheted over rocks on the path, and she brushed her blonde locks out of her eyes.

"Tatiana, isn't there anything you can do to help us get out of this and soon " Cress tried to keep her voice calm as she asked her travel companion, the fairy godmother.

Tatiana's violet eyes shut as she prayed to Hoseenu, her silver hair acting like a veil as she bowed her head in reverence. Cress tried to stifle a groan as she remembered that a fairy godmother could only use her powers if Hoseenu decreed it.

Hoseenu, please help us! Cress herself prayed. *And it would be really appreciated if You did it soon,* she couldn't help but add.

Cress peeked out of the carriage's window and caught a glimpse of several men on horseback starting to close in on the carriage. As she was about to pull herself back from the window, she was startled to see a tree root seem to jump out of the ground and trip one of the men's horses. She turned to look at Tatiana, who had opened her eyes and was smiling in satisfaction.

"Was that soon enough for you " Tatiana grinned.

Cress's mouth dropped and she stuttered as she replied, "Yes."

"Watch out!" She pulled Cress to the floor of the carriage. An arrow was now sticking out of the back of the seat that Cress had just been resting against.

"Thank you." Cress's voice shook.

Tatiana nodded as they both got off the floor. "It was a lucky shot on their part. They should all have been tossed from their horses by now, so we'll be out of their reach shortly."

They sat in silence as the driver slowed the horses to a less grueling pace.

Cress had known of inherent risks traveling from Lyra to Wilderose. However, when she had accepted the invitation from Queen Sophia of Wilderose to come to the Wilderosian court, raiders attacking travelers along the border had been far from her mind.

Her best friend and the Queen of Lyra, Ravenna, had reminded her of the dangers, but Cress had brushed it off as unnecessary worry. Not that she said as much to Ravenna since her parents the former king and queen of Lyra had been murdered by raiders on this very route. The man behind the raiders was dead. Wilderose and Lyra were working together to get rid of them now that Liam, the Second rince of Wilderose, brother to Queen Sophia of Wilderose, had broken the curse over Ravenna and tied their two kingdoms together in marriage.

In the end though, Cress had reassured Ravenna that she would be safe since Tatiana was also coming with her. Even though they would not travel with guards, Ravenna couldn't argue against the fact that a fairy godmother was the best protection a mortal could have.

Fairy godmothers were rare and dedicated to Hoseenu as well as whichever family they were tied to. The royal family of Lyra had been blessed to have centuries with Tatiana, and now that Liam was part of the family, Wilderose would benefit from Tatiana's magic just as Lyra did.

Cress glanced over at Tatiana. She wondered if Tatiana ever regretted becoming a fairy godmother.

All fairy godmothers had been born human, and no one but fairy godmothers knew how to become one, but wasn't it lonely living centuries just to watch loved ones grow old and die without you

Then there was the reason behind Ravenna's curse Garrett. He had broken Ravenna's heart by requesting her hand in marriage, but then drunkenly revealing on the night before their wedding that he had never loved her. He had only loved her throne. It wasn't until Liam bore the brunt of the curse by living life as a dog until he and Ravenna truly loved each other that Garrett came back to help them with the raiders. Cress hated that Garrett had turned out to be useful in their hunt for the ring leader. Even though Ravenna was now happily married to Liam, Cress still had a hard time forgiving her friend's former fiancé. But it didn't matter now she had left him to do whatever he needed to do and would blessedly not have to deal with him for at least three months while she was off in Wilderose.

A week after the raiders' attack, and two weeks since they had started their journey, the Wilderosian castle finally loomed just ahead of the carriage. What a delight it was to behold! espite living in the Lyrian castle for several years, Cress had never imagined that another castle could be so tall. It sat with high rising towers on all four corners, in the middle of a sparkling lake. The towers appeared to touch the clouds as the sunlight reflected off their windows. Liam had told Cress some of Wilderose's history before she left, including that the castle was built during a time of unrest.

Liam and Queen Sophia had both talked about the architectural feat of their home, but she realized that she must not have believed them when they told her. How could they, or anyone, live in a piece of art It was surreal that she was even able to see it for herself. After Ravenna and Liam had gotten married,

Liam's older sister, Queen Sophia, asked Cress to come and design dresses for the Wilderosian court. It was a dream come true for Cress. The wedding dress that she made for Ravenna spurred the Lyrian nobility to commission her, and now she was finally starting to visit new countries and learn more about their fashions.

Cress could just make out the outer edge of the Elven Wood behind the castle. The trees were always green even the ones whose leaves usually turned colors in autumn. It was rare for someone outside of Wilderosian descent to enter those woods, and she hoped that she would be counted as one of the few lucky foreigners during her stay.

Upon arriving at the castle, Cress couldn't wait any longer inside the carriage after being cooped up for two weeks. She got out to finally stretch out her long legs as soon as it stopped moving. Tatiana chuckled behind her, but Cress didn't care. This was the farthest away from home she had ever been, and therefore the longest she ever had to endure the confines of such a small space. part of her was relieved that their stay was going to last for at least three months. She would need the time to mentally prepare for the return trip.

"Welcome to Wilderose!" a voice called out to them. Cress turned to see that it belonged to Queen Sophia of Wilderose, currently striding toward them.

Cress grinned and replied, "Thank you! It's so good to see you again, Sophia!" She hugged the foreign monarch despite the gasps coming from the dignitaries that trailed behind the queen.

Sophia laughed. "I'm so glad you're here, Cress. and you as well, Tatiana," she said as she reached out to hug the fairy godmother.

Tatiana smiled, hugging Sophia in return. "I'm delighted that I get to work with you and the Wilderosian crown again."

As servants hurried about, Cress and Tatiana followed Sophia through the giant wood doors at the end of the courtyard. Cress's mouth dropped at the sight of so many elven art pieces on display. Despite the fact that she had only seen one or two since she had moved into the castle at yra, she immediately recogni ed its distinctive features as elven it would be hard to mistake the delicate silverwork as something a human created. The elves' metalwork was always flawless and smooth and they used only the purest of metals.

"Your family must have a closer relationship with the elves than your ancestors did when I was here last," Tatiana commented as she looked appreciatively at a rose made out of solid gold on display in one of the hallway's many alcoves.

Sophia's cheeks turned as bright red as her hair while answering. "My father decided before I was born that he wanted our two countries to be on the best possible terms. Which meant that we bought a lot of their art during our visits to the lven Wood."

"Visits? As in many?" Cress asked in delight. Sophia nodded. "We're still in good standing if you want to visit during your stay here."

Cress nearly ran into a silver figurine of a swan, she was so focused on making sure that Sophia was making a serious offer. "I'd love to!"

Sophia's smile strained a bit as she replied, "I'll send out a letter to see if it is possible." Turning her head to look at Tatiana she added, "I can see if you would be welcome to come as well."

"I would also like to visit," Tatiana said. Though she replied without almost knocking over a priceless piece of art.

It was then that Cress noticed they had stopped in front of a door next to the swan figurine.

"Cress, this will be the guest suite that you'll stay in. I hope you like it." Sophia gestured to the door. Before Cress had even opened it, Sophia turned to Tatiana and said, "I can show you to your room. It's right this way."

"Before we go, Cress and I wanted to let you know that our carriage was attacked by raiders on our way over," Tatiana told Sophia. The queen blanched. "Are you alright? Do you know where it was?"

"It was just after we crossed the mountain pass and along the border," Cress interjected. Quickly she added, "Tatiana and Hoseenu kept us safe." No need to worry Sophia about the arrow that had almost pierced Cress.

Sophia sagged in relief. "I will let the soldiers know that the raiders are still active. I thought that since Ravenna's uncle was no longer supplying them information they would have dispersed. I see I have been too optimistic."

Cress winced at the mention of Ravenna's uncle's involvement with the raiders. It was still a sore spot for avennabecause she was still working out how to keep her cousin Irena safe from the backfire.

All while dealing with Irena's unpleasant attitude towards avenna. Cress conceded though that Irena was still grieving the death of her father, even after the discovery of his traitorous ways.

Sophia addressed Cress, saying, "Since you probably both want to rest tonight to recover from your harrowing journey, I'll have the lady's maid assigned for your stay bring a tray up around dinner time."

"Thank you. I'll look forward to dinner, but I don't need a lady's maid." Cress brushed off the idea with a wave of her hand.

Sophia tilted her head to look at Cress, "Maybe not usually, but you are my guest here and I want to make sure that you are well taken care of while I'm in meetings." She grinned as she added, "Which unfortunately is more often that I would like." And with that, she turned and led Tatiana up the hallway.

Cress shrugged and walked into her temporary new room. As soon as she saw it in full, she gasped. It looked almost as big as the king's and queen's chambers back home in Lyra. It was definitely a lot larger than her own room. She took a few steps into what could only be described as a parlor sitting area and spun around to catch a glimpse of everything.

All of the white furnishings had pale green accent pieces. Any fabric that covered the furniture was a patterned blend of both. The vaulted ceilings highlighted a glass chandelier. This was a room for a princess - not a dressmaker.

Before she could fully recover from her awe, a quiet knock followed by the sound of the door slowly opening came from behind her. She quickly turned around to see a short young woman with light brown curls, startling grey eyes, and a matching grey dress that had a white pattern throughout.

The woman curtsied and said, "Hello miss. I am to be your lady's maid, and I have brought you some dinner." The lady's maid set a tray on one of the tables in the parlor.

"Hello. You can just call me Cress," Cress quickly offered her name. Before she had left Lyra, Ravenna had reminded Cress that in Wilderose, names were sacred and citizens only shared their names with each other when the person of a higher station shared theirs first.

The lady's maid grinned, "Thank you for offering your name. Myname is Yetta."

"Thank you for offering your name, Yetta," Cress smiled in return.

"Once you finish your dinner, I will draw up a bath while your things arrive. They should be here shortly."

"That sounds lovely, but I can do that. You don't have to actually wait on me." Cress tried again to protest the need for a lady's maid, but just like with the queen, she failed to convince Yetta as well. Yetta just waltzed into the bathing room, leaving Cress with her dinner. It was a simple affair of bread, cheese and some fruit, but Cress ate it gratefully.

Cress stepped out of the bathing room feeling refreshed. She noticed that while she took her bath, Yetta had laid out Cress's nightgown on the bed and left the room. That was when it finally sunk in that she was in Wilderose as a professional dress designer. She had worked her whole life to get to this moment!

Overcome by giddiness, she squealed as she ran and jumped onto what was now her bed. It absorbed her impact as she sunk into the plush mattress.

Giggling, she prayed out loud, "Thank you, Hoseenu, for this! I can't wait to see what else You have in store for me while I'm here!" She finished getting ready for bed and tried to sleep, despite feeling extremely excited about what lay ahead.

CHAPTER 2

Garrett was getting really tired of snow. If he were to take a guess, his horse would probably agree with him. They were being pelted nonstop by the stuff with no sign of stopping. Despite the Lyra-Wilderose mountain pass being nowhere near as high in elevation as the mountains to the north, snow still remained, even in the middle of spring. It was one of the reasons he had gladly left his post at the border to be a personal guard for the queen of Lyra. It hadn't mattered that he had previously been engaged to said queen; anything was better than snow.

He looked up to see how much farther he had to go until he would reach the next outpost. It was the last one along the border, and he had been dreading it because it was the one that he had previously been stationed at. The thought of being back at the place of one of his biggest regrets was so nauseating that even though it made the most sense to the outpost where he had interacted with the raiders, he had hoped that he could get information from somewhere else.

He had been one of the soldiers that was paid off by the raiders to look the other way. He justified it to himself that they never hurt anyone. They just took from the wealthiest of travelers who could always afford the loss. He didn't know that they were planning on murdering the former king and queen of Lyra. The monarchs he had sworn to protect and serve as a soldier of Lyra.

All of the guilt from their deaths resulted in him unable to use the gold that he was paid for his indiscretion. Then to top it off, someone knew that he was, indirectly, responsible for the king's and queen's deaths. He was blackmailed to cover up his mistakes. It wasn't until he was back at the capital acting as Queen Ravenna's bodyguard that he was able to fess up what he had done. Now he had to finish making everything right, or rather, as right as they can be after irreversible harm was done.

Sooner than he would have liked, Garrett reached the settlement's gates. He looked up at the lookout towers and half hoped no one he knew was there. On the other hand, it would sort of be a relief if there was - he would at least be let in out of the cold faster.

"Why, if it isn't the would-be king! What an honor it is for His Majesty to visit us out in the mountains."

Garrett grimaced as he heard one of his old comrades shout down at him. He quickly schooled his face into a playful grin. "Aye, and your king would like to get out of this blasted cold. Open up already, Seamus!"

Garrett thought he heard Seamus snicker rightbefore the gates opened wide, but he wasn't sure. He nudged his horse forward. He dismounted, and a short man with thick brown hair running down into a matching beard came up and clasped Garrett on the shoulder.

"Good to see ya, mate!"

"It's only good to see me because you don't have to keep looking at your own ugly mug anymore."

Garrett turned to the man who gave out a bellowing laugh.

"You haven't changed a bit, Your Majesty." The man said the latter part with a flourishing bow. Garrett made sure to keep his smile in place at the moniker.

"Sorry I can't say the same for you, Seamus," Garrett replied with a laugh as he patted the man on the back. Hoping to ease him up so he was more willing to share any knowledge he had with Garrett.

"Well, we can't all leave this frigid wasteland, now can we?" Seamus said. "Now let's get your poor horse taken care of and get you inside."

The two men bantered while they walked toward the stables. As they joked back and forth, Garrett was still able to take in all of the coordinated chaos around him. Men and women went about their daily responsibilities. Some practiced in the training yard despite the cold, while others patrolled along the outpost's walls.

After leaving his horse with a groom, Garrett followed Seamus toward the mess hall. The main building was a favorite among the soldiers who lived here. Not only was the food served here, but it was the warmest one - there were constant fires stoked to cook over no matter the time of day. It allowed every shift to have a regular meal while also making sure that no one froze to death.

Garrett hated being back.

"Now, what *actually* brings you here?" Seamus asked as they sat down at one of the few smaller tables in the large room. He barely finished his question before gulping down some of his stew.

Garrett stared down into his bowl as he stirred his spoon around the unrecognizable clumps before answering, "You remember our, uh, friends?" He looked up just in time to see Seamus stiffen.

"Aye."

"I need to..." Garrett took a moment to think on how to phrase his sentence, "...reconnect with them. I'm a little low on funds and could use our friends' help."

Seamus relaxed and said, "Well, you're no longer going to find them here. They've moved closer to the Wilderosian capital. I might know a way for you to get ahold of them if you want to travel outside of Lyra."

Garrett gave his first genuine smile of the day. "I'm all ears."

CHAPTER 3

Cress followed Yetta to the royal family's private dining room. She had woken up early due to all of the excitement, but quickly realized that she had no idea where she was supposed to meet everyone. Right as she finished getting dressed, her door opened, and there was Yetta explaining that she was to accompany Cress to breakfast.

"How long have you been working at the castle?" Cress asked.

"A couple of years." Yetta brusquely answered.

Cress waited to see if Yetta would say anything more, but when the lady's maid didn't elaborate, Cress tried a different question. "Have you lived in Wilderose your whole life?"

Yetta only nodded with an affirmative hum.

Cress gave a quiet sigh before speaking up again. "Is everything alright?"

At that, Yetta abruptly stopped walking and turned to look at Cress, brow furrowed. "I think so. Do you think there's something wrong?"

Cress could feel her cheeks heating up as she fumbled with her words. "Well, it's just that I was worried with the short answers you gave; I thought there was a problem."

Yetta's eyes widened. "A lady's maid is not supposed to talk about anything other than her duties."

At that Cress gave a little snort. "We're going to have to change that. Conversations can't all be boring, now can they?"

Yetta's lips turned up into a small smile. "No, I suppose they cannot. I've lived my whole life in Wilderose, but when I turned fourteen, I left home to find work at the castle."

Cress grinned, "See? That wasn't so hard! That means that we're close in age. I started working at the castle in Lyra when I was twelve, but that was almost six years ago."

Before Yetta could reply, Tatiana caught up with them from behind and said, "Good morning, Cress. How did you sleep last night?"

Cress smiled at the fairy godmother and said, "The little I had was restful, but I'm just too excited about being somewhere new. What about you?"

"I could have probably slept through an earthquake; I was out as soon as I lay down."

Tatiana turned toward Yetta. "Hello, I don't believe we've met."

Yetta gave a quick curtsy. "I'm the lady's maid assigned to Cress, Your Grace."

Tatiana smiled at the young maid. "You may call me Tatiana. Hoseenu knows everyone does."

Yetta blushed and looked down before whispering, "Thank you for offering me your name. You may call me Yetta."

Cress had forgotten what it was like to feel nervous around the fairy godmother. She remembered of course that Tatiana had been the one to offer Cress a position at the castle, and how anxious she had initially felt being around the most powerful being in Lyra, if not the whole world. But that had subsided rather quickly once she saw how often the fairy enjoyed tea and cookies with the Lyrian castle's cook. If Cook wasn't scared, then why should she be? Later she would reassure Yetta that Tatiana wasn't someone to worry about.

As they continued walking together toward the breakfast hall, Cress noticed something. "Do you not have a lady's maid with you?" she asked Tatiana.

"As helpful as I'm sure Yetta is to have around, I wrote to Sophia that I do not need assistance."

Cress opened up her mouth to object to being the only one in the awkward position of being served despite her class, but stopped short when Tatiana gave a slight shake of her head before nodding toward Yetta.

"This is her first time being able to serve a royal guest. If she does a good job with you, she'll be given a raise," Tatiana whispered.

Cress looked over at Yetta, who pushed open a door and then stepped aside to allow her followers entry.

"I see," Cress said, and walked through the open

door where she found Sophia serving herself a plate at a buffet table.

"Good morning!" Sophia cried out when she saw that her guests had arrived. "I hope everything is to your liking."

Both Tatiana and Cress expressed that they were happy with their rooms as they made their way over to the food table. With the three women seated, the nearby servants exited the room to leave them alone with their breakfasts.

"I thought that after we finish eating, I could give you a tour of the castle and the grounds," Sophia said.

"That sounds lovely," Tatiana replied.

Cress nodded her head since she had already filled her mouth with a bite of food.

"Then at some point, we should discuss actual business. Especially because I would love to talk more about hosting a ball not only to honor working with a fairy godmother," she looked over at Tatiana, and then turned to address Cress, "but to also give you a chance to showcase the new styles that you design while you explore Wilderose."

Cress straightened up in her chair and quickly swallowed, but before she could say anything, Tatiana said, "A ball like this seems very strategic." She knowingly took a sip of tea and looked over the brim of her cup at Sophia.

Sophia gave a wry smile and answered, "We're still dealing with the raiders, and it will encourage my people to see that one of our strongest allies is going to support us."

"I can see how honoring Tatiana is important, but I

don't see how this needs to include any of my clothes," Cress interjected.

"Cress, you are Queen Ravenna's closest mortal friend and someone who is making a name for herself in her own right. Having a famous Lyrian dressmaker work on designs inspired by Wilderose would be a symbol of our countries working together to stop the raiders."

"When are you hoping to have this ball?" Cress asked. She took a sip of her own tea as she started thinking about how much time she would need to prepare.

"How much time will you need to make a dress for me and outfits for five members of my council?" Sophia asked.

Cress choked on her tea. Tatiana reached out and thumbed back. Immediately Cress was able to take a clear breath and smiled in thanks at Tatiana. She told Sophia, "I'll need three months to design and make them, but that's only if I have a team of seamstresses to help. I would handwork yours, of course."

Sophia nodded. "I've already made sure to set a team aside for you. The only thing I needed to know was how long it would take."

"I guess it's settled then," Cress said.

"Wonderful. Now, let's finish our dinner so we can go on the tour of the castle!" Sophia exclaimed before taking another bite of her breakfast. Cress and Tatiana looked at each other and smiled as they followed suit.

CHAPTER 4

The market was filled with patterns. Everywhere Cress looked, people wore bold patterns on their clothes. The butcher had animals on his tunic, while the florist had blue flowers decorating her skirts. Even the banners above the fruit sellers had images of their wears decorated throughout. Cress spun around with a wide grin on her face, trying to catch sight of all the varying adornments.

Lyrian fashion was more about the cut of the clothing, and generally kept to a monochromatic color scheme. Wilderose had the most basic of styles, but made up for it with intricate pattern arrangements. She would have to figure out where they got their fabric. They were an agricultural country with their fields and rich soil.

"If you're not careful, you might end up getting pickpocketed."

Cress immediately froze mid-spin at the sound of *that* voice. She looked to her right, where the voice had come from, and sure enough - there stood Garrett. The sun reflected off of his black hair; his green eyes shone in amusement. He stood leaning with his arms crossed against the post of one of the seller's stands, which belied how much taller than her he actually was.

"What are you doing here? Shouldn't you be near the border tracking down raiders?" she said, ignoring his opening statement. She had known there was a possibility of seeing him but was annoyed that he showed up on her first day exploring.

"I'm following a lead here in the capital. Imagine my surprise, running into a fellow Lyrian in Wilderose," Garrett said as he straightened up and closed the distance between them. Cress had to tilt her head back to actually look at him eye to eye. There weren't many people taller than Cress, and it irked her that his height always threw her off balance.

"Well, I guess I shouldn't distract you from your work then," she said, and started to turn away when Garrett reached out to grab her hand.

"Cress, wait. It's been a while since I've talked with anyone about anything other than finding these blasted raiders' hideouts. Can't we at least catch up a little bit?" Garrett smiled down at her as he basically begged her to stay.

Cress bit her lip as she looked around before settling back on his face. "I'm staying at the castle with Liam's sister. I can ask for you to be let in to visit after dinner," she started, but then smirked and added, "if you're still desperate for company by then." Cress doubted he would go out of his way to meet her. So she was surprised when he beamed and said, "I'll be there.""Oh." He must have been more desperate for company than she had realized. "I'll see you later then. Goodbye." Cress hurried off with only one glance behind her to see Garrett still standing where she left him, watching her go.

Garrett watched as Cress hurried in the direction of the castle. He had been surprised to see her in Wilderose, but felt an unexpected relief at finding a familiar face. Even if it was a face that was annoyed at seeing him. Since leaving Lyra shortly before Queen Ravenna's and King Liam's wedding, he had been busy trying to redeem his wrongs. There hadn't been much time to think about anything else.

He smiled as he remembered the time spent with Cress looking for answers behind the Lyrian nobilities' accidents. She was fi lled with life and it drew him toward her. Her beauty didn't hurt either: tall with blond hair and blue eyes and a quick mesmerizing smile.

Garrett shook his head trying to clear Cress from his mind. He was at the market for a reason, and despite the fact that he enjoyed spending time with Cress, she wasn't the type of woman that he usually went after. She was too focused on what she wanted from life instead of just looking for a good time. "More like you're not the type of man that she would be drawn to, " he muttered to himself as he strode toward one of the nearby taverns.

The tavern sign read "The Pig's Blood Tavern." Garrett hoped that the "pig's blood" part of the name was not because it was an ingredient in the tavern's specialty drink. After a moment's hesitation, Garrett pushed open the door and strolled through.

The first thing he noticed was the smell. It was a mix of ale, sweat, and urine. Looking around the dining hall, Garrett could see that the patrons of the crowded tavern looked like they hadn't bathed in years. *That explains the smell*, he thought.

The tables and chairs looked like they'd been repaired so many times that it was no longer worth fixing any slants or uneven legs. It was like everything and everyone no longer cared about being a functioning part of society.

Despite how packed the place was, Garrett immediately recognized a man he knew. He hid a grimace as he sauntered toward his previous contact with the raiders. The man set his drink down on the table when he looked up and saw Garrett approaching him.

"Well, well, well... if it isn't Mr. High and Mighty himself. Take a seat." The man gestured at the empty chair across from him. Garrett reluctantly sat down.

"You're far from home aren't you, Your Majesty?" The man drawled the nickname Garrett had earned during his time in what felt like exile, but was really just a few months at the border. He resisted punching his contact when a barmaid came up to their table to ask him what he would like to eat or drink.

After she left with his order, Garrett took a deep breath, which he instantly regretted as his nostrils filled with the stench of the tavern, and said as he leaned closer, "I'm looking to make some extra coin."

His companion took another sip of ale before he asked, "Is that so?"

Garrett stayed quiet. From past experience, it was better to say only what you needed to. Anything more could be used against you. It wasn't until after the man had downed the contents of his tankard that he spoke again. "You'll have to go ask for opportunities yourself this time."

Garrett frowned. "What do you mean?" He didn't even glance over as the barmaid came back with his own tankard; he was too focused on the conversation at hand.

"I mean that I'm leaving Wilderose within the month. I'm not staying to be your keeper."

"If you won't talk to our..." Garrett paused as he tried to think of a euphemism, "...friends, then how am I supposed to 'ask for opportunities' myself?"

The man grinned, displaying his yellowed teeth. "Luckily for you, I know the perfect person to introduce you to. I think you'll like her. Everyone does," he said with a wink.

"Her?"

"Aye, her. She'll be coming into the city in a few weeks. Now that I know you're here, I'll find you when she arrives. I'd work on your wooing skills if I were you. She's easier to handle when men dote on her."

Garrett leaned back before asking, "How is *she* going to help me make coin?"

"Rumor has it she's the only one who knows where our friends' current... dwelling... is located."

"You don't know where they are?" Garrett rubbed a hand over his face. This conversation was supposed to be one of the more straightforward ones of his investigation.

"Nope. I have my own keeper. The paranoid lot," The man said then spat on the ground next to him. "Speaking of, I'm supposed to meet him now." He gave Garrett a pointed look.

Garrett took the hint. He got up without saying anything else and left. Once he got outside, he took in a deep breath of the fresh air, glad to be out of the dark, dingy tavern. With some time left before dinner, he decided to go back to his inn to freshen up.

Garrett smiled when he thought about seeing another familiar face. Although this time, a much prettier face than the one he had just left inside.

CHAPTER 5

After dinner, Cress sat on one of the armchairs in her room with a piece of paper and a stick of charcoal. She had wanted to jump in immediately and start drawing out different designs inspired by her trip to the market, but had to wait until after she spent time with her host.

She hadn't made much progress when she heard a knock on the door. Sighing, she got up to open it.

"Oh," was all she could think to say when she saw Garrett with a lazy grin on his face.

His grin grew wider as he asked, "Can I come in?"

She blinked a couple of times, but then she registered what he said. "Yes, of course." She stepped aside so that he could walk past her. After closing the door, she turned to see him admiring the room.

She narrowed her eyes. "What are you doing here, Garrett?"

He turned to meet her gaze. She could see a hint of mischief in his eyes. "It has been a while since we last saw each other, and I haven't gotten my reimbursement from our investigation."

As soon as he said that, Cress knew he was referring to the time they had helped Ravenna and Liam find out who was behind the deadly accidents in the Lyrian court. It was what lead them to discovering that Ravenna's uncle was behind the happenstances.

"Excuse me, but I paid for all of those bribes!" Cress sputtered out.

Garrett smirked. "But if it weren't for my presence, you wouldn't have gotten the information we needed."

Cress's mouth opened in retort, but closed when she found she couldn't think of anything to say.

Garrett walked right up to her, causing her to crane her neck back to look at him. He commented, "I think this is truly the first time I've ever seen you speechless."

Stepping back, she finally responded, "If reimbursement is all you're looking for, then I can offer you some coin." Cutting Garrett off from his reply, she asked, "What did your lead say today?"

He scowled. "Nothing useful. At least not for another month." He held up a hand when she opened her mouth to ask a follow up question. "That's all I can share until then." This time, his trademark smirk was back in place, "Looks like you get to have more time with me."

"I thought you only wanted payment, which

you'll have before you leave. I've got nothing else that you want."

"Shouldn't I decide that?" he said as he stepped forward again and closed the gap between them. This time she held her ground and lifted her chin up as he commented, "You're the prettiest sight I've seen in ages."

Cress rolled her eyes. "I'm sure that's not true."

Garrett leaned down closer. "I can assure you that it is."

Garrett was halfway out the door when Cress called out after him, "Wait! Your coin."

He paused in the doorway and said, "I'll just come back tomorrow and get it." Then he winked at Yetta and closed the door behind him.

"That insufferable knave!" Cress growled at the closed door.

Yetta giggled, "He seems to be a handsome knave." Cress looked over at her lady's maid. "Don't you dare tell him. He has a big enough head as it is."

"I'll be sure to keep my mouth shut tomorrow when he comes back to visit you."

Cress groaned and flopped onto her bed while Yetta continued laughing.

Garrett chuckled to himself as he walked out of the Wilderose Castle. Cress was just too easy to rile up. It had been the same way when they were kids. Although, she seemed to not realize that he was the same weaselly little kid from her childhood.

When he first spotted Ravenna at the market and saw that she was friends with Cress, he had been worried that Cress would recognize him, which would have made his plans to woo the princess a lot more difficult. However, she had never said anything, so he continued to pretend that he actually had a reputable enough background for a queen's suitor.

It wasn't until a couple of years later when Ravenna had forced him and Cress to work together while they were trying to solve the mystery behind the court's accidents that he realized she truly did not know who he was. He had tested the waters by mentioning her mother's old shop, but she just asked him how he knew about it. He had lied and said something about her reputation as a dressmaker, including the fact that her mother used to own a tailor shop in the Lyrian capital city. It was enough to get her to drop the matter.

Garrett frowned. He didn't know why, but it bothered him that Cress didn't remember him even though he had recognized her immediately. People usually remembered meeting him, it was just how things went. Of course, Cress *would* be the exception to that rule. She always seemed to have her own standards on how the world worked.

Shaking his head, he continued on toward his inn where he would be able to finally be able to rest for the first time in months.

CHAPTER 6

"I hear you had a handsome visitor last night," Sophia said at the breakfast table.

Cress shot Yetta a glare, but Yetta held her hands up as if to say, "It wasn't me."

"The guards here are the worst gossips," Sophia chuckled. "They mentioned that a soldier from Lyra had stopped by to visit the Lyrian dressmaker."

"What's this about Garrett?" Tatiana asked as she sat down with her plate of food.

Cress groaned and said, "Garrett is here in the capital of Wilderose following up on the raiders' hideout." She caught sight of Tatiana and Sophia sharing a smile. "What?!" she demanded.

"Where is he staying?" Sophia asked.

"I don't know. I didn't ask him."

"You should have him stay at the castle. Anyone

investigating those rogues should at least have a comfortable stay while they're here," Sophia insisted.

"I don't think that's a good idea," Cress said.

"Nonsense. I insist. Wouldn't you agree, Tatiana?" Sophia looked over at Tatiana who was drinking a cup of tea.

"I think that sounds like a good idea."

Cress's mouth dropped. "I thought you didn't like him," she accused Tatiana.

"I never said I did not like him. I just didn't think that he and Ravenna would be good together." Tatiana's violet eyes twinkled.

"Then it's settled, when he visits again, you need to ask him to stay here," Sophia said before moving on.

Cress ate the rest of her breakfast in pensive silence. She still had a lot of work to do in preparation for the ball in three months. Garrett would not get in the way of that. She'd make sure of it.

Cress was in the gardens when Garrett found her this time. Before he let her notice him, he took some time to watch her examine the different plants. Her blonde hair glistened in the sunlight. She leaned over a bush to get a closer look at the shrub's flower. He realized she had a piece of paper that she was sketching on as she observed.

"I didn't realize you were into plant life," he said as he came toward her. Cress gave a little shriek as she spun toward him. He couldn't help but laugh.

"It's you," she said after a moment of catching her breath.

He smiled, "Yes, it's me."

"Well, since you're here, I might as well get this over with," she seemed to mutter more to herself than to him.

"What's that?" he asked.

She looked heavenward as she sighed, "Queen Sophia has requested that you be her guest here at the castle."

"I'm sorry, come again?" Out of all the things she could possibly have said, that was at the far bottom of the list.

She looked at him reluctantly. "Since you are helping look for the raiders' hiding spot, she wants to extend an invitation of hospitality as a means of thanks."

His mouth twitched as he tried not to smile at her monotone delivery of what sounded like a very rehearsed request. "I'd be delighted to stay at the castle." This time he did let himself smile as she sighed dejectedly. Despite Cress's clear reluctance to extend the invitation, he wasn't going to miss an opportunity to trade the inn life for the luxurious palace life. It didn't hurt that he would be with familiar people around him.

"I'll let Sophia know. You'd best be getting your things from wherever you're currently staying," she said before going back to sketching one of the flowers.

"I thought you were a dressmaker, not a gardener," he said, completely ignoring her advice.

Cress looked back at him. "I'm creating a dress for Sophia for a ball in three months, and I have an idea to incorporate a flower pattern. Specifically her favorite flower, or at least a variation of her favorite flower." She pointed down at the flower in front of her. It was a blue stargazer lily with five white triangular petals that met in a blue middle. Cress continued, "Her flaming hair would go well with blue and white, so that's why I'm drawing this specific flower."

Garrett had no idea what she was talking about, but it seemed to no longer matter. She had stopped as if remembering who she was talking to.

"Shouldn't you be getting your things?" she said again, making it clear that she wasn't asking so much as telling him.

"You seem eager for me to move in."

She just shrugged her shoulders and went back to drawing, a clear dismissal if he ever saw one. Instead of continuing to fight for her attention, he decided it'd just be quicker to grab his few possessions from the tavern and then come back to try and get a reaction out of her. Her obvious dislike of him made it more amusing for him when he was able to get under her skin.

CHAPTER 7

Over the course of the next several weeks, a pattern emerged. Cress would wake up and have breakfast with Sophia and Tatiana. Then she'd either explore the city to get more inspiration or sketch out new ideas in her room. She had gathered all of the councilmembers' measurements and gave them to her own team of tailors. Some designs had even been ready for her to draw out patterns for them to work on.

It was still hard for Cress to believe that she was the head tailor over this project, and every time she remembered, she would quickly squeal out a prayer of thanks to Hoseenu for the opportunity.

Garrett had also become a semi-regular fixture in her life. An annoying fixture, but he was there nonetheless. He would drop by every so often at different hours of the day for a variety of reasons. If she didn't know better, she would think that he actually liked her.

However, she did know better. Whenever he decided to walk with her through the city, she would catch him flirting with different women, some of whom he'd make plans to meet up with later. She started playing a game with herself to see if she could lose him for the rest of the day whenever he got distracted by another woman. Once she got rid of him, she would go about her business as usual.

More often than not though, he'd eventually find her even if it had been over an hour since she had last seen him.

"How do you keep finding me?" she asked one time after he had located her in a fabric store. She planned to order fabric to embroider for Sophia's dress. The design finally looked amazing on paper, so it was time to start prototyping.

"I'm a Lyrian soldier. We are trained to track our quarry."

She wanted to punch him in his smug face.

That had been yesterday, and she hadn't seen him around since then. It was now time for dinner. It was special in how *not* special it was. The last few nights, Sophia had had to host several dignitaries from Harmon. They had left this morning, so now she was free to spend a quieter dinner with Cress and Tatiana in the smaller royal family dining area.

"How are you both liking your stay in Wilderose so far?" Sophia asked her two guests when they had all sat down to eat.

"It's been great!" Cress exclaimed as she picked up a slice of bread to butter. "I've been able to see so many different styles throughout the city and make different patterns that I think are going to be a great mix of Lyrian and Wilderosian fashion." She finished by taking a bite out of her bread.

Sophia set her fork down and leaned back in her chair as she looked at the seamstress. "Cress, what do you do for fun outside of work?"

Cress's brows furrowed. "What do you mean?"

"I mean just what I said. For example, when I have time off from my royal duties, I like exploring or reading. It relaxes me."

Cress looked over to see what Tatiana would say, but the fairy godmother continued eating as though the conversation wasn't happening.

"I, uh, don't know," she finally admitted.

"I don't want Ravenna to think that I'm working her friend to the bone," Sophia teased, but Cress could see that the queen still seemed concerned despite her playful tone.

"I'll make sure to let Ravenna know that I'm happy here and to not worry about my leisure time," Cress chuckled.

Sophia only smiled in reply and continued eating. Thankfully, Tatiana changed the subject, asking Sophia how the visit with Harmon went. Cress kept up as much as she was able, but for some reason, she couldn't get Sophia's question out of her head.

CHAPTER 8

Garrett waited inside the rancid Pig's Blood Tavern for his contact to introduce him to the woman who supposedly knew where the raiders were located.

He took another sip of his ale and considered leaving. It had already been an hour, and still no one had arrived. He set his tankard back down on the table and had just scooted his chair out to get up when he saw a woman with blood red hair walk in and stride right toward his table. Startlingly beautiful with piercing grey eyes, she wore a scarlet dress that matched her hair. When he stood up next to her, he discovered that she was even taller than him.

"You must be Garrett." Her voice was deep and sultry, and he barely concealed the shiver it sent through him.

"And you are?" he said after clearing his dry throat.

She gave him a lazy smile as she sat down at his table. "Willow."

Garrett quickly followed suit, sitting opposite of her. He briefly glanced behind her but didn't see his contact, so as much as he wanted Willow to be the woman he was supposed to meet, he still wasn't completely sure.

"Looking for someone?" she asked as a barmaid brought her her own tankard of ale.

"I'm supposed to be meeting someone here, but I don't see him," he trailed off.

"I think you are referring to our mutual friend?" she asked as she took a deep sip.

Garrett only nodded. There was something about Willow that kept him on edge. He was used to being the one in control during these sorts of interactions, and this was one of the few times when he was not.

"He said to tell you that he was called away early." She paused as she leaned forward to look at him, almost like a cat eyeing a mouse. "And that you were supposed to keep me company while I'm here."

"Oh," was the only brilliant reply he could think of. That's when he noticed it: the sleeve of her dress had pulled back when she reached for her drink, and she had a black spider tattooed on the underside of her wrist.

He mentally cursed. Of course the woman that would know where the raiders' hideout was would be a witch.

Witches became more addicted to their sorcery the more magic that they used. Magic that was fueled by human lifeblood. How crazy were these people if they were willing to work with someone like Willow? And who knew how she would respond to the slightest of insults, let alone a betrayal of trust? Which was what he had been planning on, just to get her to tell him where the raiders were located. This was going to end terribly for him.

"I have just the place in mind for us to spend in each other's company." Garrett tried to recover himself with a suave smile.

Willow's eyes lit up as she replied, "Where were you thinking?"

"Have you ever been to the outskirts of the Elven Wood?"

CHAPTER 9

Cress had finally started working on her first prototype of Sophia's dress. She loved that everyone in Wilderose wore diff erent patterns on their clothes instead of one solitary color per gown like was the custom in Lyra. It challenged her to not only think of the style of clothing, but also how the pattern had to be laid out within that style. Now she just had to combine patterns with an intricate style of dress. A perfect blend for the Queen of Wilderose whose brother was the King of Lyra.

As she walked around the mannequin that Sophia had provided for her, pinning fabric together to see how it would look, she couldn't help but think about what Sophia had said at dinner. Did she work too much? She hadn't thought so...she had fun with her friends when time allowed for it. Granted, her only real friend was

Ravenna, and she was busy running a kingdom alongside her new husband. And even though she would have called Tatiana her friend, this was the first time in a long while that she had actually spent significant time with the fairy godmother without Ravenna nearby. She could now say that she was friends with Sophia since they had spent more time together during her visit, and then there was Yetta, who was slowly opening up to Cress. She had friends! Besides, she loved her work and finally having the freedom to design and make anything that she wanted.

Cress took a step back to look at the mannequin. The fabric was a floral pattern, and she had wanted the skirt to also look like a lily's bloom, but there was just something not right about it. She sighed as she started to unpin everything and fasten the fabric in a different layout.

Hoseenu knew how much her career meant to her. She had come from the slums of Lyra's capital. Even though her mother had had her own mending shop, she wasted so much of her potential on Cress's father, a man who Cress had never met. Despite loving her mother greatly, Cress knew she wasn't going to repeat her mother's mistakes. She was going to, and already was, making a name for herself. She thanked Hoseenu that His chapel servants had taken her in after her mother's death. If they hadn't done so, she never would have been able to find work at the castle mending the other servants' socks. It was where she met and became friends with Ravenna. Cress wouldn't trade any of that for anything in the world. Other than maybe more time with her mother.

The skirt still wasn't cooperating. She huffed as she again took out the pins holding up the fabric. Cress tried to think through all the different ways that could make the vision she had of this dress become reality. After a while, she found that a headache had formed behind her forehead and she could no longer concentrate on the fabric. Heaving a sigh, she looked out the window and saw that the sun had long since sank beneath the horizon. It seemed like it was time to be done anyway. She'd try again tomorrow.

As she got ready for bed, she rang for a servant to bring up a cup of chamomile tea. She hoped that the tea would soothe her headache before she fell asleep. As she waited for the tea to come, she leaned against the window to see the moon shining down on the Elven Wood. Maybe she could prove Sophia wrong - she could have some fun by asking Sophia to visit the outskirts where humans didn't need special permission to enter.

She heard a knock on her door and made her way over to open it, expecting to find a servant with her tea. However, when she opened the door there wasn't a tray containing her warm beverage.

"Garrett, what are you doing here?" Cress asked. The sight of the handsome soldier at her door made her painfully aware of the fact that she wore just her nightgown. She crossed her arms over her chest as she waited for him to answer.

"May I come in?" Garrett said with an easy grin. Cress reluctantly stepped back to give him space to walk into her room.

"You didn't answer my question. What are you doing here?" she asked again.

Garrett took a slow look around the room and stopped to focus on the mannequin with the unpinned fabric draped over it. "I thought I would stop by to say hello before I leave tomorrow to follow a lead."

Cress scowled, but when she opened her mouth to say something, Garrett interrupted as he walked over to the mannequin. "I don't know much about fashion, but I thought that the fabric was at least supposed to be sewn together." He picked up a piece of fabric and held it up to his chest, giving her a cheeky smile.

"Give me that! It's not finished yet," Cress growled as she quickly snatched the fabric from his hands.

"No need to bite my head off." Garrett raised his hands as he stepped away from the fabric.

"What do you *want*, Garrett?" Cress ground out as she placed the fabric back on the mannequin. Miraculously, it actually laid out nicely this time.

"As I said, I just stopped by to let you know that I'll be following a lead on the raiders' whereabouts."

His words finally sunk in. She looked back at him. "You mean you found out something new?"

He smiled, her least favorite smug grin, as he crossed his arms and looked down at her. "I did."

She closed her eyes and took a deep breath through her nose. "Are you going to tell me what you found out?"

Garrett's smile grew bigger to show off his white teeth. "Nope."

"Why not?" Cress resisted stomping her foot. She would not let him make her act like a child.

"Maybe because I only want to tell you when I have something more definite to share with you."

She let herself indulge in rolling her eyes. "You're actually going to be spending time with a woman, aren't you?" It wasn't a question.

Garrett jerked his head back. Almost as if she had physically slapped him in the face. "Why would you think that?"

"Because that's what you always do. You fl irt with women and act like you could have just been chasing skirts this whole time. What's worst is that whoever this woman is, she'll have no idea that you're just going to be using her for your own gain."

"Is that what you truly think about me? That I'm some rake who only thinks about his what he can get from people?" Garrett frowned, and this time Cress did not see any amusement anywhere on his features.

"Am I wrong?" She met his eyes with a steady gaze. Instead of replying, Garrett strode out of her room, leaving her alone amidst confusion.

Garrett stormed out of Cress's room and headed toward his own room farther down the hall, almost bumping into a stand holding an elven sculpture of a swan. He didn't know why, but it irked him that Cress thought he wasn't serious about stopping the raiders. Sure, he liked women, and he would be lying if he said he did not chase after them for a good time. That did not mean that he did not take his responsibilities seriously. And of course he needed to use his leads! He had to learn more about what he was up against without tipping them off .

He banged open his bedroom door and immediately went about his room to start packing his things. Here he was, about to risk his life getting information out of a witch, and Cress just thought that he was some sort of brainless flirt.

Garrett paused what he was doing to take a deep breath. He was about to embark on a treacherous encounter with one of the most dangerous creatures in the world. He needed to focus.

Looking out his window, he saw stars filling the night sky. He didn't really remember his parents. All that he had growing up were Hoseenu's chapel servants, and they had their hands full taking care of all of the orphans in the city. No matter how much he tried to leave that part of his life behind, it always snuck up on him. Like how the chapel servants would remind the children before they fell asleep that Hoseenu loved them and to look at the stars to see how vast his creation was, just like his love.

"I know that I'm probably the last person that You'd want to hear from, but I could use Your help tomorrow," Garrett whispered to Hoseenu. Despite his earlier frustration, he felt immediate peace.

CHAPTER 10

The soft light of dawn shone through Cress's window, casting a golden glow in her room. Cress thought that it looked beautiful and wondered if there would be some way to capture that in a gown.

Maybe Sophia was right and she *was* too obsessed with her work. She had spent the whole night tossing and turning because it still bothered her that Sophia saw her as someone who couldn't stop working. Well, she would be a changed woman today and take a break!

If she was honest with herself, she was also bothered about how Garrett had left last night. She saw that her opinion of him had upset him, but she wasn't sure what else he could possibly expect her to think. He had broken her best friend's heart badly enough that she had willingly cursed herself. Cress had even seen the moment when it happened. He had kissed a barmaid the night before his and Ravenna's wedding. Then he revealed that he was just using Ravenna to become King. At least she hadn't brought that up last night; she did have *some* tact.

Giving up the hope that maybe she still had time to fall asleep, Cress dragged herself out of bed and slowly got ready. It was still too early for Yetta to arrive, which probably meant that it was also still too early for breakfast. However, Cress would rather get there early than stay cooped up in her room.

Opening her bedroom door slowly, she peeked out into the empty guest hallway. She slid out of the room and tried to quietly walk toward the breakfast hall. She didn't want to wake up anyone else who might have stayed the night. She passed by the swan sculpture and took the turn that would lead her to her destination. When she arrived, she was surprised to see Sophia already standing inside, holding a cup of steaming tea as she looked out the breakfast room window. Even though you couldn't see it from the castle, the Elven Wood lay in that direction.

"Good morning," Cress said.

Sophia spun around and almost spilled tea onto her dress. "Oh Cress, good morning. I wasn't expecting anyone to come in so early."

Cress smiled. "Couldn't sleep either?"

Sophia gave a wry smile of her own. "Not really. I want to apologize to you."

Cress tilted her head as she waited for Sophia to continue.

"I shouldn't have implied that you were only spending your time working, and I'm sorry. You've taken up this task of making gowns for a ball that you didn't even know was going to happen. I'm grateful for your willingness, but I think I got worried that maybe you were not enjoying yourself." Sophia bit her lip.

Cress shuffled her feet. It was the first time that Cress had witnessed the Queen of Wilderose look unsure of herself, and it honestly made Cress slightly uncomfortable.

"You were right. I think I have been working too hard for a very long time." Cress gently smiled as she saw Sophia exhale in relief. "In fact, I was going to suggest taking a break today and possibly going to the outskirts of the Elven Wood."

Sophia tensed briefly before putting on what looked like a forced smile. Cress wasn't sure why, but Sophia didn't seem to like talking about the Elven Wood. So Cress quickly added, "I can just go on my own for the day."

Before Sophia could respond, Tatiana walked into the breakfast room. "Where do you want to go by yourself?"

Both the queen and dressmaker looked over at the fairy godmother. Cress answered, "I was just telling Sophia that I could use a break and would like to see the Elven Wood, or at least the parts that are open to humans."

Tatiana looked first at Cress and then at Sophia. She nodded to herself as if she had made some sort of decision. "I think you'll enjoy yourself. However, I was hoping to steal Sophia for the day to ask her some questions about Wilderose's agriculture."

"I'll make sure that you have a guard to escort you to the woods," Sophia said to Cress. Cress looked over at Sophia who seemed to have relaxed considerably.

"That's alright. I don't need guards, just a horse. It's not like I'm anyone recognizable."

Sophia frowned, but before she could say anything, Tatiana spoke up, "I think you'll be better off without a guard. Just remember that no matter what happens, Hoseenu is always with you, and if you need anything, all you have to do is ask Him to send me."

Cress again glanced over at Sophia to see if she understood any better than herself, but from the confused look on the queen's face, she seemed just as lost as Cress felt. When Ravenna and Cress were younger, Ravenna sometimes complained that Tatiana wouldn't give her straight answers. Maybe this was what she was talking about. Cress shrugged and said, "Oh, alright. I'll remember. Thank you, Tatiana," before they all sat down to eat breakfast.

CHAPTER 11

The horseback ride to the Eleven Wood from Wilderose's capital took three hours. Three hours of thinking about all of the work she still needed to get done before the ball that was just a month away. So much for enjoying her day off.

Cress halted her horse right before the woods' entrance. All around her on the ride over were fields and meadows with a few hills here and there. That all stopped abruptly in the face of looming evergreen trees. From what her human eyes could see, there was only a single trail leading in and out. The foliage off the trail was too thick to walk through.

It occurred to her that maybe it wasn't such a good idea to enter another world alone. From what Sophia had told her, there was no possible way for someone to accidentally walk into the part of the forest where the elves lived. Their magic saw to that. As well as making sure humans were kept safe from wild animals. But now that she was here, she was no longer sure that she would not be treated as an intruder walking around the non-magical part of the woods. It felt more magical than the woods in Lyra ever had.

Well, she was here now and she would not waste those three hours of traveling just to turn tail at the entrance. Taking a deep, steady breath, she nudged her horse forward and down the path, praying to Hoseenu to keep her safe.

After a couple of minutes, she was amazed at how the shadows disappeared and that sunlight seemed to shine through the tree line despite how dense it had seemed from the outside. There were even more paths that opened up around her, and she was thankful for the compass and map that she had brought with her so as to not get lost.

When her stomach growled, she looked for a spot to eat a late lunch. She could hear water running somewhere off to her right, so she turned her horse toward the sound. The path she was on led her to a small creek which she decided to follow downstream. She was glad that she did because the creek ended in a small lake with a clearing on the other side. Deciding to eat lunch at the clearing, she kept going on the path that wound around the lakeside.

When she reached the small meadow at the edge of the lake, she was surprised to see she wasn't alone. She was even more surprised to see that she recognized one of the other individuals as Garrett.

Keeping Willow at ease was a lot more work than Garrett had first thought. She was just waiting for an opportunity to use her magic. Especially if it meant using it on him. Already he had had to assure her that he would be the most proper of gentlemen if they were to ride on a single horse. She had demanded full permission to turn him into a frog otherwise. Then while they were exploring the Elven Wood, she had wondered out loud if he would make a beautiful tree. He tried to convince her that he would not.

It was starting to look like he would have to gain her trust over multiple outings before she would reveal the raiders' location. He seriously considered looking for an alternative method of finding their hiding spot if it meant not spending he did not have to spend more time in the presence of a witch addicted to using black magic and cursing people at the drop of a hat.

It was finally time to eat the lunch that he had brought for them. He figured that she would be too distracted to curse him if she was busy eating. At least, he hoped that would be the case.

They found a lake with a meadow on one side of it that would be a perfect setting for lunch. Garrett pulled out the food from their saddlebag, as well as a blanket for them to sit on. Once he had laid everything out and made sure the horse had taken a moment to drink some water, he tied the reins to a tree branch nearby and sat beside Willow.

"So Garrett, what made you decide to bring me to this lovely forest?" she asked him.

To make sure we weren't around other humans you could curse if things turned out badly, he thought to himself. Out loud, he said with a warm tone, "Your beauty needed a deserving backdrop to enhance it."

Willow threw back her head and laughed. Garrett held his breath to see if it was a good laugh or one that would be a sign of doom for him.

"You truly are a flirt." She smiled at him before taking a bite out of an apple.

He let out his breath, but tried not to scowl at the word 'flirt.' It was all too close to what Cress had said the previous evening and everything else Cress had implied. Instead, he smiled and said, "I only speak the truth, m'lady."

As soon as those false words left his mouth, the sound of someone arriving on horseback interrupted any response Willow might have had. Both Garrett and Willow looked over at one of the paths along the lake and saw a chestnut mare with a rider. Garrett hoped that whoever it was would pass by quickly. He couldn't be responsible for a passerby getting cursed for showing up in the one spot he thought no one would be around.

Garrett squinted to get a better look at who was atop the horse, only to feel the blood drain out of his face at the horror of seeing Cress. Of all the people to have found them, of course it had to be someone who actually knew him. And much to his chagrin, someone who didn't fall for his charms.

His hope that maybe he could get Willow to leave with him as soon as possible was dashed as soon as he heard Cress say, "Garrett, what are you doing here?"

Holding back a groan, he stood up from the picnic blanket that he and Willow ate at and said, "I'm dining with the lovely Willow." He gestured toward the red-haired woman frowning at Garrett.

Cress dismounted her horse, walked straight up to him, and poked him hard in the chest with her finger. "I *knew* you weren't actually going to be working, but rather with another conquest. What are you planning on using her for?"

Fortunately, she didn't mention anything about the raiders. Thank Hoseenu for small mercies.

Cress continued poking him. "*This* is why I said what I said last night about you 'chasing skirts!' And to think that I stayed up all night worried that I had offended you."

Garrett opened his mouth to speak, but Cress continued talking. "For Hoseenu's sake, *swans* are more faithful than you! At least they mate for life."

"Swans, you say?"

Garrett's heart started to beat faster and he could feel sweat dripping down his forehead when Willow spoke up.

Turning toward the other woman, Cress said, "I'm so sorry miss, but anything this man has told you was a lie. You don't want to be with him."

"Is that right?" Willow's tone was calm and steady, but Garrett saw a predatory gaze in her eyes.

He tried to catch Cress's eye and convey that they were in danger, but she just continued ranting to Willow.

"He broke my friend's heart the night before their wedding, and he uses people mercilessly."

"Is this true?" Willow asked him directly.

Garrett closed his eyes and prayed that somehow this wouldn't turn ugly. "I was engaged to her friend, yes." He was not going to admit anything else.

"Sounds like you need a lesson on being faithful." Willow stood up and stalked toward him. Automatically, Garrett stepped in front of Cress. He heard Cress gasp softly behind him, and then she whispered, "Is that a spider tattoo on her wrist?"

He nodded and kept his eyes on Willow, who was standing right in front of him now. Then Cress did one of the most foolish things that Garrett had ever witnessed. She stepped out, placed herself in front of him, and said to the witch, "I actually think he doesn't need any lessons. He's been quite focused on his work as a soldier of Lyra, but is taking time away to travel. Who wouldn't want to spend time with someone as beautiful as yourself on their day off? And he was just being friendly with those other women. Nothing untoward, I can assure you."

Garrett could tell that Cress was starting to ramble, but to what end?

"Cress," he whispered as he placed a hand on her arm to get her to stop.

"Actually, my dear, I think he does need a lesson, and it seems like you are the perfect person to help him learn."

"Cress, run! Now!" Garrett shouted as he pushed her toward her horse.

"Not so fast," Willow said evenly, right as she shot a bolt of magic from her hand at the horse, causing it to turn tail and run away. Then she focused her gaze on the two of them.

"Since swans mate for life, it seems only fitting that you should be one." She spoke to Garrett, but then she looked at Cress who seemed frozen in her tracks, eyes wide in fear. Garrett realized that he couldn't speak or move his legs, no matter how hard he tried. "You will share in his fate by being his mate. If you leave him by choice, which will allow you to turn back into a human, or by death, or if he leaves you, he will die of a broken heart."

Cress started shaking her head back and forth as tears spilled from her eyes. Garrett once again tried to move toward her, but he couldn't. He was still stuck. Then Willow's magic hit him and Cress, and the world started to grow.

CHAPTER 12

Cress's view had shrunk significantly. The cattails towered above her, and while the trees surrounding the lake had always loomed large, the extra distance between her and the treetops was daunting. She briefly wondered if this was how Ravenna felt having to look up at everyone around her.

A hissing noise drew her attention back to Garrett and the witch. The witch had tried to pet the top of Garrett's head. In response, Garrett spread out his new wings to make himself bigger and let out a hiss, trying to scare the witch off. Instead, she just laughed at him.

"Seems like you're adjusting well to your new form, my pet. Don't forget to be a good mate now, darling!" Then in the blink of an eye, the witch was gone. Garrett lowered his wings and let out a small groan.

"Are you alright?" Cress asked automatically. She

was surprised that she was still able to speak. At least the curse allowed that much. Garrett only bobbed his head in reply.

"Can you speak?" Cress cautiously asked. The witch had been angry at him specifically. Cress was just unfortunate enough to be around at the time.

"Yes?" Garrett looked relieved being able to speak that one word.

"Good. Now, what were you thinking?!" Cress yelled at him as she waddled over to where he stood. Now that she knew that he could speak with her, she was finally going to demand some answers out of him.

"Everyone knows that witches become more addicted to their magic with each spell that they cast! What in Hoseenu's name possessed you to court one?" Cress was now an inch away from Garrett's face. Her eyes flashed in fury.

"I was trying to get information from her!" Garrett shouted back. "She somehow knows where the raiders are hiding out. I was trying to learn where their locations are!"

"And the only way you could have done that was by wining and dining her?"

"No, but it was the least suspicious way."

"Admit it, you just wanted another notch in your belt. It must have been nice to brag to all of your friends that you were able to get a kiss from a witch after getting a princess to fall in love with you."

Garrett narrowed his eyes at Cress.

"Oh, yes. I just love boasting about all of my conquests to friends I haven't seen in over a year!" He threw up his wings in exasperation as if he still had human arms. If Cress wasn't seething right now, she would have laughed at such an odd sight.

"And now I get to tell everyone that I've been turned into a swan and gotten stuck with the most annoying little dressmaker as a mate. A mate that if I abandon, I'll die of a broken heart, just like a real swan. I'm sure that'll make everyone jealous."

"Oh, I'm sorry!" Cress rolled her eyes. "It's not like I asked for this either."

"Are you sure about that? Because if I remember correctly, I was about to gain valuable information before you jumped in yelling about how much of a flirt I am!" Garrett hissed.

For once, Cress didn't have anything to say in reply. She just tilted her head to look at the swan before her. His black eyes narrowed and she noticed that he had unintentionally unfurled his white wings to make himself look bigger.

Letting out a sigh she said, "What's done is done. We should try to figure out a way to get word back to Tatiana and Queen Sophia about what happened. Maybe we could fly there if we could figure out how to use our wings?"

Garrett tucked his wings back at his side at her change of tone. "It's hunting season right now. We'll just end up as targets. Besides, we don't even know if we can fly."

An uncomfortable silence fell between them. Cress ruffled her new feathers and kept readjusting her wings as she waited for Garrett to say something. Instead, he just turned away from her and headed toward the lake.

"Where are you going?" Cress asked him.

Garrett paused and looked back at her. "I'm going to look around for a spot for us where we can be safe. I need to make sure you don't die." Then he continued waddling toward his intended destination, leaving Cress alone.

Hoseenu, help me, she silently prayed. Garrett had paddled out of sight around a bend in the lake, so she couldn't tell if he had found a place for them to stay.

She closed her eyes and let out a deep breath. That's when she remembered Tatiana's odd comment from this morning. Her eyes snapped open. Had Hoseenu told Tatiana that this would happen?

Hoseenu, we need help. Can you ask Tatiana to come find us here? she prayed. A gentle breeze stirred up around her, and when she closed her eyes, it almost felt like the brush of someone hugging her.

When she opened her eyes, she saw Garrett heading back toward her. "Did you find a place for us?"

"I did. Come on, we can swim over now and eat on the way." As soon as he mentioned eating, Cress felt hunger pains in her belly. She thought of the food in her pack that she had left with her horse. The sound of rustling feathers startled her out of her musings, and she looked up to find Garrett waiting for her. Without saying anything, she walked to the lake and got in.

Floating on top of the water was such a strange sensation. She had no fear of sinking, and with the barest kick of her webbed feet she moved forward. Garrett had followed her in but had moved in front of her to lead her to where they would make camp.

Her stomach rumbled and she realized that she hadn't eaten anything since she had left the castle that morning. The next thing she knew, she had started to dip her head under the water and grab some of the underwater vegetation with her beak. She quickly raised her head out of the water and swallowed the little bit of food she had managed to pull up. It was also in that moment that Garrett turned around to look at her with his head tilted.

"What are you doing?"

"I, um, I was hungry?" she said as if she were asking a question.

"Huh," was all that Garrett said, and then he too dipped his head under the water and came up with pieces of plants that he quickly gobbled down.

Cress wasn't sure exactly what exactly was happening to them, but she just prayed that their curse was different from Liam's in that they wouldn't also have to worry about losing their humanity on top of everything else. Maybe their new swan bodies were just acting on instinct.

Maybe flying won't be as much of a challenge, she thought. That would actually make this curse worthwhile. Having a literal bird's eye view could give her so much inspiration for Wilderosian fashion.

"You coming?" Garrett called.

Cress shook herself out of her thoughts and back to the present. Garrett had reached the bank of the lake and waited for her to catch up. Her feet eventually touched the bottom, and she walked out of the lake and continued to follow Garrett to a little alcove of trees.

She waddled around, looking at the space. It was at

that moment that the events of the entire day hit her, and she felt exhausted.

"I think I'm going to take a nap," she told Garrett.

"As long as it's where I can see you, that's fine," Garrett said as a way to remind her that if something happened to her, he was as good as dead himself.

Cress walked over to some tall grass at the edge of the lake and plopped down. *Hoseenu, please help us,* she prayed again, and then twsited her long neck around her body and fell asleep.

CHAPTER 13

Garrett kept watch over Cress while she slept. They were swans...how were they supposed to get out of this alive? Liam, the only other person he knew who had also been transformed by a curse, had at least been a predator when he had been turned into an animal. He and Cress were birds. Prey.

He was pleased though that unlike Liam, at least they had a voice. It was petty, but there was not a lot of good about their current situation. He would take what he could get.

Looking over at Cress, he wasn't sure who he was more upset at: Willow, Cress, or himself. His first instinct was to blame this all on the witch, but really, he shouldn't even have tried to get information from her to begin with. He should have tried a different method of finding the raiders' location from the start, because chances were good that he would have ended up cursed even if Cress hadn't shown up when she did. Now Cress had been cursed too, and it was all his fault. If only he had told her what he was doing, then she wouldn't have been as quick to get mad.

If only you hadn't given anyone reason to believe that you are such a flirt, he thought bitterly.

Stuck ruminating in "what ifs," Garrett hadn't heard anyone approaching until someone said, "Hello, Garrett."

Startled, he let out an embarrassingly loud honk as he swiveled his neck toward the voice. He saw Ravenna's fairy godmother standing next to him.

"Tatiana?" Garrett looked behind him and saw that Cress, who must have been startled awake by his honk, had gotten up and came to greet the woman in front of them.

"Hello, Cress. Hoseenu heard you asking for help, so here I am." She smiled at the two swans.

"Can you reverse this?" Garrett, forgoing his manners, cut in.

Tatiana's smile dropped. "I'm sorry, I can't. But I can make it so that you both can break it on your own."

Garrett didn't think that swans were expressive by nature, but Cress looked the closest to crying that he had ever seen a swan be.

"How?" Garrett snapped, but tried to calm himself down. He had already offended one magical person, he really couldn't afford to make another one mad. "I'm sorry, but how is it possible for that to happen?"

Tatiana sat down on the grass so she could be closer to their eye level. Reaching her hands out to both of them she asked, "May I?" and placed them on both Garrett and Cress when they nodded their heads. She said, "The only way for you to become human again, and break the curse, is by creating each other.

a gift made from suffering. This witch wanted you to suffer, so that is how you will break the spell. You must weave together shirts made from the stalks of stinging nettles and present them to one another. To accomplish this task, you will become human at night, but only if you are near this lake."

As she spoke, Garrett saw a soft glow leave her hand and entered his whole body. A warmth filled him. When he looked over at Cress, he saw that the same thing was happening to her as well. Looking back at Tatiana he saw that the fairy godmother was starting to sweat and sway a little where she sat. As soon as she finished speaking, her eyes shut, and she slumped down. Garrett could hear her breathing heavily.

"Tatiana, are you alright?" Cress cried out. The fairy godmother slowly opened her eyes and gave a wane smile. "I'm alright. Your witch friend was just a little bit more powerful than I expected."

"Come over here and lie down," Cress said as she gestured a wing out toward the flat area in their alcove.

"I'm fine. Really, Cress. Besides, Sophia should be here soon with supplies you'll need, and we'll need to help you both set them up before we leave while it's still daylight."

He knew it took three hours by horseback to get to the Elven Wood from the Wilderosian castle. They hadn't even been swans for a full two hours, yet Tatiana was here, which he decided was probably because she was a fairy godmother. And somehow Queen Sophia was going to arrive shortly with supplies that must have taken some time to arrange. "How does she even know to bring them?" Garrett asked.

Tatiana's smile brightened. "Let's just say I had a hunch."

Cress groaned. "Is that why you were being so cryptic this morning?"

Tatiana didn't answer her, but instead silently stood up and walked toward the clearing on the other end of the lake.

"We might as well join her since it's probably where we'll meet up with Sophia," Cress told him.

"Is she always like this?"

Cress snorted, "More or less." She got into the water and started swimming. Garrett quickly joined her.

CHAPTER 14

By the time the two swans reached the clearing, Sophia had arrived along with several of her guards and a wagon full of supplies. She was talking with Tatiana. Sophia looked over their way and immediately came toward them.

"Cress, I am so sorry. If I had known that this would happen, I'd never have let you come by yourself. Ravenna is going to be so upset when I tell her. She trusted me to keep you safe."

"Don't tell Ravenna!" Cress practically shouted.

All eyes turned toward her and Cress knew that if she were human, her cheeks would have turned red.

"I have to tell her. She and Liam are going to be coming in a month for the ball."

"She's been busy getting everything ready for her new school system and dealing with everything else involved with being queen. I don't want to add this to her plate."

Sophia opened her mouth to say something, but Cress interrupted her. "If we're still swans by the night of the ball, then we can let her know. But until then, we keep this to ourselves."

"I could just cancel the ball," Sophia said curtly.

Cress shook her head. "No you cannot. It's important."

"A major part of the ball was to showcase your outfits to symbolize Lyra's and Wilderose's unity to stop the raiders. That can't happen if you're a swan."

"My team is working on the designs of your council's garments. Your dress was the only one that I was working on entirely on my own."

"Which you still cannot work on as a swan." Sophia leaned back and crossed her arms.

Tatiana cleared her throat, causing everyone to focus their attention on her. "Actually, I made sure that this was packed." She pulled out from the wagon a large chest that contained the floral dress that Cress had been working on the night before, as well as her mannequin.

Sophia threw her hands up in the air. "Fine. We won't cancel the ball." She stalked toward the wagon in frustration.

Cress giggled as she watched Sophia order her guards to set up everything that Cress and Garrett would need for as long as they were cursed.

Tatiana walked over to her. "I'm sorry to say this, but human food wasn't included," Tatiana whispered to Cress, who abruptly stopped laughing.

"It's alright. We can eat as swans," Garrett piped up

after being quiet for so long that Cress had honestly forgotten that he was with them. He must have overheard Tatiana and noticed Cress's reaction.

"That's what I thought," Tatiana said.

Cress saw that Garrett kept adjusting his wings as if he couldn't find a comfortable position for them.

"Are you alright?" she asked him when Tatiana had walked back to the wagon.

"I'm not used to just watching others set up camp instead of doing it myself," he grunted.

By the time Sophia and Tatiana left, the sun had started to set. Cress looked around her new home. There was a large tent set up near the tree line portion of the meadow. Inside, she found sleeping mats and bedding on opposite sides of the tent. The mannequin with Sophia's dress sat near the middle back. On the outside of the tent on the side closest to the lake, Tatiana had made a fire pit with several logs and kindling so they could see while they knit.

After she finished exploring, Cress waddled toward the edge of the woods where she saw a patch of nettles. If they were going to break free of this curse, she might as well start collecting the plants they'd need to weave their shirts.

Cress threw her head back and strode toward the plant. She stopped in front of the nettles and she bent her neck to get a better look at her wings as she realized there was no way for her to use them to pick them.

Grimacing, she reached forward and used her beak to pull up one of the plants. As soon as the nettle touched the inside of her mouth, she felt the sting of the leaves. She wanted to drop it, but she hadn't quite gotten it out of the ground. As soon as it was up, she rushed as quickly as she could to the lake and took a deep gulp of water. She was sure that if she were human, tears would be strolling down her cheeks.

Before she could go back and pull more, a voice cried out, "What do you think you're doing?"

Cress looked up and saw Garrett coming toward her. She raised her head and said, "I'm starting to work on breaking the curse," trying to show as much bravado as possible without revealing how much pain she was in.

Garrett stepped out of the lake and shook off the water from his feathers. "It can wait for when we have hands."

She wilted a little as she realized that she could have saved herself some trouble. So she changed the focus off of herself. "Where have you been?"

"I wanted to see the whole lake. It's going to be a nightmare keeping predators away."

Cress shivered when he said "predators." With everything happening so suddenly, the association between swan and prey had not crossed her mind until this very moment.

However, before she could give a response, Garrett started to glow. She looked down at herself and noticed that she was also glowing. Then in a flash, she saw that they were both human.

Laughing, she ran up and hugged Garrett, "Tatiana's spell worked!"

Garrett also let out a laugh as his arms wrapped around her. "Did you doubt that it would?"

"I hadn't thought so, but apparently I did." She looked up at Garrett who was smiling down at her.

"I did too."

Realizing that she was still in his embrace, she quickly pulled away and looked down, letting out an accidental shriek as she did so.

"What is it?"

"This...this...dress!"

Garrett pulled back to get a proper look at her. "What do you mean?"

"It's hideous! It's an insult to all dresses that have ever come before it!" Cress pulled up the skirt so she could give Garrett a better look at the monstrosity that she wore.

It was a white strapless dress, which would not have been that big of a problem on its own, but it was covered in swan feathers. Attached to the back of the dress was a long veil that looked remarkably similar to folded wings. Then at the very bottom edge of the skirt, the dress became orange. Her shoes were a matching orange. It didn't even make sense. Their feet were black when they were swans.

Cress took a proper look at Garrett, groaning, "And your outfit isn't any better."

Just like her dress, his shirt and trousers were covered in swan feathers and complete with faux wings on the back of his shirt. The worst was still the orange, only instead of the edge of his trousers, it was the boots that came up to the middle of his shin.

"*This* is what made you scream like a banshee?" Garrett asked incredulously.

"I'm a dressmaker. I would rather be a swan than have to wear this dress. I hope that this was from that witch's magic. Not from Tatiana's. Otherwise, I'll be very concerned about her."

Garrett shook his head. "I think it has been a long day and we should get some sleep."

"But what about gathering nettles?"

"That can wait until tomorrow night."

Cress crossed her arms over her chest. "How about you go to sleep, and I'll pick nettles. I want to break this curse as fast as possible."

"Please don't. I'd rather have an extra day being cursed than for something to happen to you while I sleep," Garrett said with his eyes closed.

Cress dropped her arms to her side and tilted her head as she looked Garrett up and down. Every part of him seemed to sag in exhaustion. Her heart went out to him and she said, "How about you go sleep while I work on Sophia's dress by the fire next to the tent."

Garrett only nodded and shuffled inside. He was already lying down on one of the bed mats when Cress went in to grab the dress. Then shortly after she built up a fire before the last of twilight's radiance faded, she heard gentle snoring come from the tent.

"Hoseenu, why did you let this happen? I don't know about Garrett, but life has already been hard enough for me. You know this, so why?" Cress looked out at the darkening lake and let herself feel her despair.

CHAPTER 15

Garrett woke up to the sound of songbirds. Despite their objectively pleasant morning greetings, he wished that he was still asleep. Especially because it was still dark outside.

He rolled onto his side and looked over at the other bed mat. Cress was curled up on her side, clutching her blankets close to her. He peeked at the mannequin at the foot of her mat and saw that she had made a lot of progress since yesterday.

Taking a deep breath, he rotated onto his back and slowly exhaled, getting up as quietly as he could and stepping outside.

There was a hint of sunlight in the east, so it wouldn't be long before they both turned back into swans. Garrett considered for a moment if he should wake Cress up now or let her sleep through the transformation. He decided to let her sleep for now as he walked up to the edge of the lake. He knelt down and splashed some water onto his face, hoping it would make him feel more awake. It didn't.

The rustling of the tent flap told him that he no longer had to worry about whether or not to wake Cress up. He continued facing the lake as she walked up beside him.

"I'm sorry," she said.

He turned his head to look at her. She wasn't looking at him, but out onto the water.

"For what?"

"For rushing in yesterday and calling you a flirt. Among other things." She finally looked up at him and gave him a small smile before she continued, "I should have believed you when you told me that you were following a lead."

Garrett barked out a humorless laugh. "Why should you?" All day yesterday her words had haunted him. He *had* spent time with other women while he was engaged to Ravenna; he would flirt and try to see what could get from them. It wasn't like Cress was wrong to imply that he was faithless.

"Because finding the raiders was the only thing you were guaranteed to be serious about. I saw it last year after you admitted to being blackmailed and we worked together when you were trying to right your wrongs. This is important to you."

Garrett started to reach out to hold her in his arms, but before he could do something so foolish, they both started glowing. He quickly looked east and saw that the sun had fully risen. The next thing he knew, they were both swans again.

"Well, it doesn't matter now," he said, and paused before continuing, "but thank you."

Cress bobbed her long neck up and down in acknowledgment. Then she said, "Hungry?"

He snorted and followed her into the water to eat lake weed again.

It was only midday and Cress was bored. It turned out there wasn't a lot to do when you're a swan. They were only able to swim around and occasionally break up the monotony by eating. She hadn't spoken to Garrett again since apologizing that morning. Not because she didn't want to talk with him, but because she had no idea what to say. She still felt awkward about the whole mess that they were in, and it had dawned on her last night while she was sewing that her life was not tied to his. She really could leave him, and even though he would die, she would still be alive.

She shuddered at the thought of the witch making it so she could turn human at the expense of Garrett's life. It was not something that she wanted to test. Thankfully, Tatiana had given them a definitive way to become human again.

After swimming yet another lap around the lake, she decided it was time to try flying. She swam toward

Garrett who was resting on the lake shore. His long neck wrapped around his body, but he angled himself in such a way that he could still see the lake. She briefly wondered how long it had taken him to figure out exactly the right way to face when he laid his head down.

When she was almost to him, he lifted his head slightly.

"How about we give these wings a test run?" She lifted her wings to show them off.

Garrett was quiet for a long time. Cress gradually lowered her wings back down and waited for him to say something. Anything.

"Alright."

"Really?" she gaped at him. She had actually expected him to mention hunters again.

"We should be fine if we just stick to this area. I asked Sophia about hunters, and she said that humans aren't allowed to hunt in the Elven Wood, even the parts where they can easily come and go."

"That's wonderful news! Let's go try now!" she crooned, and waddled out of the water.

Garrett's beak opened in what she knew from experience was an attempt at smiling. They both made their way toward the part of the clearing away from the tent.

"Ladies first," Garrett said as he held his wing out in an open invitation.

"Scaredy cat," she said as she passed him.

"I think you mean 'scaredy swan,'" he yelled after her.

Cress chuckled, but then when she made it to the open field, she stopped to consider exactly how she was going to fly. She had only seen swans floating on the water or already in flight. She had never actually witnessed one taking off.

She glanced at Garrett who was waiting for her, then looked back at the stretch of grass in front of her. *Here goes nothing*, she thought and unfurled her wings. She started to flap them up and down, but she stayed on the ground. As she continued flapping her wings however, she found herself starting to run. Her feet left the ground shortly after.

Before she could shout that she was flying, she lost focus and ended up falling the short distance she had gained to the ground.

Garrett ran toward her with his wings outstretched for balance, shouting, "Are you okay?"

"Yes." Cress managed to say as she tried to right herself.

She squinted her eyes as she looked at the distance from where she was back to where she had started. Lowering her head, she started to flap her wings again and run. This time she kept at it, and she found herself at the height of halfway up one of the large maple trees in front of her.

"Cress, turn!" Garrett yelled.

Shifting slightly down to her left, she felt her whole body turn as she just barely missed hitting the tree. She kept flapping as hard as she could, and when she made it over the lake water, a wind caught up under her wings and kept her afloat.

A chirp escaped her beak as she started to glide. She was really flying!

The sound of another pair of wings beating caused

her to look briefly next to her. Garrett had caught up with her and they started to fly in sync. It was one of the most incredible experiences of her life.

Eventually, Garrett started to shift downwards. Cress nearly asked him to stay up with her, but then she caught a glimpse of the setting sun and followed him. He aimed his body toward the lake and landed on the water. Cress copied him.

They had just made it when all of a sudden they were two humans in the middle of the lake. Cress yelped as she went from floating on top of the water to sinking below the surface. She quickly swam up and broke through the water's surface and started laughing. Her grin stretched out as far as it could go. "That was amazing!"

Garrett was treading water next to her. He too had a huge smile on his face. "I can't believe we actually flew."

"I know!" Cress pushed back some of the wet hair that had gotten onto her face.

"Come on, we need to start a fire and get warm."

The two swam back to the shore, and Garrett went straight to the wood pile. Cress twisted her long hair and squeezed out the water, and then did the same to her hideous dress so she could at least enter the tent without dripping water all over everything.

Inside the tent, she opened the trunks that Sophia had brought. It had been too dark to see their contents by the time she went to bed last night. There was still enough light out right now so she could see if there were any towels for them to use to dry off. What she was really hoping for were spare clothes so she didn't have to keep wearing the swan dress.

She chortled when she discovered a trunk filled with clothes. Once she finished changing into a dry dress, she stepped back outside and handed Garrett a towel.

"There are some dry clothes for you too." She nodded her head in the direction of the tent.

Garrett smiled and went to get changed himself.

Cress sat by the fire Garrett had built. She kept thinking about how remarkable it was to fly. Everything had seemed so small down below them, and she felt that if the mountains weren't between Wilderose and Lyra, she would have been able to see her country.

A pang of homesickness hit her suddenly. She had been so busy this last month getting everything ready for the ball, and then yesterday being turned into a swan, that she hadn't had time to really think about what she had left behind.

"You're obviously not thinking about flying." Garrett sat on a stump across the fire from her.

"Hmm?"

"There's no way you would be frowning if you were remembering flying," he answered.

A small smile graced her lips as she leaned forward to rest her chin in her hand. "I was thinking about Lyra."

Garrett paused for a moment, then said, "What about Lyra?"

"That I miss it. I miss home."

She watched as Garrett pressed his lips together. His brow furrowed. "It would be nice to go back."

They sat in silence, the fire crackling. After some time had passed, Garrett broke the silence.

"Were there any gloves in the trunks?"

"I didn't see any."

Garrett sighed as he stood up. "Then I guess we really do have to make a gift from suffering. Ready to pick some stinging nettles?"

Cress winced. "As ready as I'll ever be."

Picking nettles is one of the worst forms of torture, Garrett thought. They had gone to the edge of the meadow they now called home. Most of the underbrush between the trees was made up of the evil little plant.

"How many do you think we'll need to pick? Do you think we have enough?" Garrett asked as he reached over to pick another nettle. His whole hand felt like Cress's sewing needles were constantly pricking him.

Cress first looked at him, then eyed the five nettles that they had pulled, before looking back at him and raising a brow. "Definitely more than five."

He grinned. "You're small. I bet you'd only need two for me to make a shirt for you."

Cress returned his smile with one of her own. "Right, and then I'll use the remaining three to make a shirt for you."

"Exactly."

The two burst into peals of laughter. Garrett was still miserable having to touch the nettles, but at least he wasn't alone.

CHAPTER 16

The sun started to set as the two swans swam toward the water's edge, not quite ready to step out of the water. As soon as the sun's light hid behind the horizon, two humans stood where the swans had once been.

Cress looked down at herself. She knew that every night the curse's magic would change her back, but she knew that occasionally curses could start becoming more permanent. She had Liam's curse to thank for her concern.

Satisfied that she looked completely human - a human in a hideous dress that tried to look like it was inspired by a swan, but came off more like a shredded pillow - she looked up at her companion.

Garrett was also looking himself over as if he too remembered what had happened to Liam. He looked up and met Cress's gaze, smirking. "Still human. It's been a week now, maybe we should be thankful that this wasn't solely Tatiana's work."

Cress snorted, "At least Tatiana's curse on Liam made it so he could turn human indoors. It's going to rain tonight." She nodded her head up at the thick clouds that had formed. Garrett cursed under his breath and started walking toward the trunk where they had stored a canopy they found. Cress followed so she could start a fire before the rain fell while Garrett set up the canopy. She was thankful that Sophia had given them camping supplies, but that didn't mean she hated the outdoors any less. If they ever broke this curse, she would never leave civilization ever again.

Over the last couple of nights, they were able to form a big pile of stinging nettles. Cress thought that they had enough to at least get started on the shirts, once they practiced a little bit. Garrett had told her the night before that he didn't actually know how to weave, let alone knit. She would have to teach him, but there was no way that she was going to teach him using their supply of nettles. The less they had to go back and pick, the better.

Once she got the fire going, she went over to the underbrush nearby. This time she wasn't going to pick any of the wretched stinging nettles. Sadly though, she was still going to risk her fingers by breaking off pieces of thorny pinkberry bushes. To top it off, it was very annoying that the pinkberries weren't even in season, so they couldn't at least have some sort of dessert as humans.

"What are you doing?"

Garrett had just finished setting up the canopy over the fire. The fire's smoke blew toward its top, but then furled away and escaped on the side.

"I'm getting some vines to teach you how to make a shirt."

"Why not just use the plants we have?" Garrett said mischievously as he jogged over to catch up with her and then slowed down to her pace.

"Garrett, if you want to practice on nettles, be my guest, but you'll have to be the one to collect any that you'll have to replace once we actually start working on the shirts. I'm not going to touch them when I don't have to."

Garrett's eyes twinkled, but he didn't say anything.

Cress reached over toward some of the bushes and carefully placed her hands around a vine branch. She snapped the branch off of the rest of the pinkberry bush. Garrett helped until she decided that they had enough for him to at least learn the basics.

When they got back to camp, she sat down right next to him in front of the fire.

"Here you go." She placed one of the vines onto his lap.

He moved his hands away as if it were a snake.

"Come on. Pick them up. They're not going to hurt you like the nettles will." She bumped his arm with her elbow before getting her own vine.

He finally held them up and said, "Now what?"

"Now you're going to take the vine, and at the end form a looped knot." Cress demonstrated on her own vine and waited for Garrett to follow suit. "We're going to create more loops in a chain by weaving the vine through the first loop. That's what I'll refer to as a stitch." Again she showed him how it was done, and again he followed along without any sort of snark or teasing. Cress saw his brow furrow in concentration as he slowly added more stitches to his row.

After a couple more, Cress showed him how to go back over his original row to create a second row. He tried a couple of times before he was able to make it so that a second stitch could be made on the second row. As soon as he got it, he beamed up at her with one of the biggest smiles she'd ever seen. Her heart gave a little involuntary flutter.

She swallowed a few times before she was able to speak again. "I think you got it, so that's pretty much it until we have to weave the edges together to form a tube. That will form the sleeves, but we'll worry about those later."

Cress got up to grab Sophia's dress that she was working on. The ball was a month away, and she still had so much left to do. The past week was busy picking nettles and then when they couldn't bear the pain anymore, Garrett created a salve he knew from military training from some of the nearby herbs to help soothe their hands.

She hadn't made it a foot before Garrett caught her hand. This time, her heart didn't just flutter, but started pounding in her chest.

"Shouldn't we start using the actual nettles?" he asked, his eyes pleading for her to say yes.

"We will, but I need to finish this dress before the ball."

Garrett frowned. "We're both cursed. Wouldn't breaking the curse take higher priority than a silly dress?"

Cress wretched her hand out of his grasp and felt heat rising up her cheeks. "That 'silly dress' is one of the most important dresses of my career. It's kind of hard to forget that we're cursed when we're swans all day, but we have plenty of time to break it. I don't have that much time to finish the dress. Just because you don't work hard to make a living doesn't mean that I don't have to."

Garrett stood up then, and again she hated how he towered over her. "You have no idea what you're talking about," he growled. "I've worked hard ever since I was orphaned as a child in the capital's slums."

"Doing what? Conning princesses to make you king? Or doing whatever it was that you were blackmailed for?" she spat.

"That was immature ambition. I've been working hard to fix my mistakes, why can't you let them go?"

"Because I've *also* had to work hard to fix your mistakes. My best friend was never the same after you abandoned her. Then I worked hard with her to fix the situation with the raiders. On top of that, I was also orphaned in the capital slums. My ambition is how I made it out. You have no excuse."

Garrett was breathing hard but didn't say anything for a long time. Cress was just about to walk away when he said, "You got a lucky break because a fairy godmother chose you out of all the orphans staying at the chapel to live in the castle. It wasn't just your ambition."

Cress took a step back. "How do you know that?"

"The high and mighty dressmaker seems to have forgotten where she actually started from and those who helped her get to where she is now. Figures," he muttered the last part before storming past her.

Cress didn't even try to stop him as a memory of a black haired boy froze her in place.

CHAPTER 17

Wham! A mud ball hit the ground in front of Cress. It had almost hit her basket with the food her mother had sent her to buy from the market. She looked up to see a small boy, who was a few years older than she was at eight, start to scoop up more mud to make another missile. He was scrawny with dirty black hair. He always seemed to have a mischievous gleam in his blue eyes. Cress called him Weasel because of it. He seemed to like it when she did, because he would never tell her his real name.

"If you throw that at me, I'll get you back a lot worse!" she cried out to the boy. He just looked up and grinned at her. Cress could see the gaps in his smile from where his baby teeth had fallen out.

"You're a girl. You can't throw mud," the boy yelled

back as he flung the mud at her. She moved out of the way in time for it to land behind her.

Cress narrowed her eyes at him and set her basket down. She bent down to make her own mud ball, but stopped when she felt more mud globs hit her face. She looked back up and saw Weasel clutching his stomach as he laughed.

"You should see your face!" he said as he pointed to her.

Wham! She managed to hit him square in the nose and laughed as he blinked in surprise. Before he could collect himself, she rushed toward him with more mud clumps in her hands and threw them at him.

Eventually he snapped out of his daze and started running away. But as soon as he turned away from her, she jumped onto his back and started rubbing mud into his dark hair with one hand while wrapping her other arm around his shoulder.

"Get off me!" he hollered.

"Not until you say you're sorry!" Cress yelled back.

The boy just grunted as he tried to shake her off. Cress's grip tightened.

They wrestled like this for several minutes until the boy collapsed under her. "Fine. I'm sorry," Weasel puffed out.

"Good," Cress said as she got off of him. She brushed back her muddy blond locks and went back to grab her basket and go home.

"You fight like a boy," Weasel called out after her.

Cress turned around briefly, saying, "No. I fight like me," and continued walking away.

Cress slowly opened the door to the small apartment above the little tailor shop that her mother ran. It wasn't until she had reached the stairs leading to their home that she stopped to see how muddy she was. From what she could tell, there was too much mud on too many random spots on her body for her to claim that she had fallen into a mud puddle. She wasn't sure what her mother would think when she saw her.

Hoping that she could sneak through to the little washroom next to the bedroom that she and her mother shared, Cress quietly stepped through the doorway and closed the door behind you.

"There you are!"

Cress jumped and turned to see her mother standing in the kitchen with her arms crossed over her chest. "You were out for a very long time," her mother continued, looking Cress up and down, eying all of the mud that covered her.

"I got everything we needed from the market," Cress said as she held up her basket. She tried to give a big smile as if that could hide how dirty she was.

"So you did," her mother said. "You also seem to have gotten more than just food today," she added with a gentle smile.

Cress looked down at the mud covering her dress and bare feet. "I'm sorry Mama." She looked up at her mother. "But it was all that boy's fault! Weasel threw a mud ball at me and I told him that if he tried again, he'd be sorry." Her eyes flashed with indignation.

Cress's mother knelt down so she was at the same level as Cress. Using a hand to brush back the hair that had fallen over Cress's eyes, her mother said, "Darling, we've talked about this before. You know Hoseenu says that even if someone else is behaving badly, that doesn't mean that you should."

"But I was defending myself!" Cress huffed with a little stomp of her foot.

"Protecting yourself is one thing, but it sounds like you threatened him back, and now you're covered in more filth than a mud ball."

"I guess so." Cress wouldn't meet her mother's gaze as she conceded that she might have been wrong.

"Alright, go get cleaned up and I'll start making dinner, okay?"

"Okay!"

As her mother started to stand up, she began coughing, causing her to double over. Cress immediately went to her side to support her.

"I can make dinner tonight, Mama," Cress offered. "I know how."

As soon as she caught her breath, Cress's mother said, "Thank you darling. I think I'm going to just lie down for a bit."

Cress nodded as she watched her mother shuffle slowly toward the bedroom. As soon as she was out of sight, Cress quickly cleaned up and started to make some stew for her mother and herself.

Cress cut up the vegetables as she thought about how her mother's cough hadn't gotten better. The town's doctor had visited months ago and said that it should have gone away by now, but it was still there, and her mother seemed to get weaker and weaker.

After she put the vegetables into the pot above the fire, Cress looked around the room. She spied some of the clothes that her mother had brought up from her shop to work on during the night. Not wanting her mother to wake up other than to eat dinner, Cress decided that she would start the mending work on the shirts and pants that had been dropped off.

As she sat down in the chair next to the fire to keep an eye on the stew, Cress rummaged around for a needle and thread from her own little sewing basket that her mother had given her. Cress's mother had taught Cress how to sew as soon as she was old enough to hold the needle without poking herself.

Cress loved watching how something as small as a needle could be used to make beautiful clothes. It was like a magic wand that could create something truly amazing out of nothing. She looked forward to the day when she could officially start helping her mother downstairs. She longed to spend all of her time with the different fabrics and see the beautiful new styles as customers came in to get their older clothes repaired.

The sound of sizzling stew brought her out of her thoughts. Setting the mending to the side of her chair, Cress got up and used a thick pot holder to pull the stewpot out of the fire and onto the counter. Next, she got two bowls out of the cupboard and sat them on the counter. She spooned a generous helping into one of the bowls, and after grabbing a spoon, she carried it to the bedroom.

Cress slowly cracked the door open and peeked inside. She saw her mother resting on the bed that they shared. Before she could decide whether to wake her mother up or let her continue sleeping, her mother opened her eyes.

"I made stew." Cress held out the bowl to her mother.

"Thank you, darling," her mother said as she sat up in bed.

Cress walked over to her and handed her the bowl. She then ran back to the kitchen, filled another bowl of stew for herself and hurried onto the bed so they could eat together.

"This is delicious Cress, thank you." Her mother leaned over and kissed the top of Cress's head.

"I know. I'm the best." Cress grinned up at her mother who started laughing.

"Yes, you are, darling. Don't you ever forget that."

A few months later, Cress ran into Weasel again. She had been out making deliveries of clothes that she and her mother had finished mending when she heard someone shout, "Come back here you little thief!" A dark blur ran past her and down an alleyway that led to a dead end. A large man just barely followed behind. From where she stood, Cress could see Weasel hiding behind some old rotten wood. His eyes were wide with fear as he looked for a way to escape. He was also clutching a loaf of bread to his chest.

"You there, girl!" Cress spun to see the man leaning over her. "Did you see where that brat ran off to?"

Cress swallowed and tried to think of what she should tell him.

"Well?" the man demanded.

"He ran off that way," she said as calmly as she could and pointed in the opposite direction of the alley. The man took off in the direction she suggested without saying anything more to her. After he had turned the corner, Weasel slowly came out of his hiding place.

"Why didn't you rat me out?" Weasel gave Cress a side-eyed look.

Cress huffed, "You looked hungry," and then continued her journey home.

"Wait up!"

Cress continued walking, making Weasel run to catch up with her.

"Thanks," he said after walking a couple of steps next to her. Cress shrugged. Honestly, she wasn't sure why she hadn't given him away. He had always been mean to her and picked on her whenever he got the chance. But when she saw how scared he was, she couldn't bring herself to let him get in trouble for trying to find a way to eat.

After a while of walking in silence, Weasel ran off with a quick, "Bye!" leaving Cress alone the rest of her way to her mother's shop.

When she turned onto the street where she lived, she saw that a crowd had gathered in front of her home. Cress shoved her way through the throngs of people. When she finally reached the front door, she saw that it was open and a man wearing the white clothes of doctors and healers leaned over her mother who was lying on the shop floor.

"Mama?" she whispered. The doctor looked up and gave her a look filled with pity.

"Your mother is with Hoseenu, child," he said.

"No," Cress whispered and then rushed toward her mother. "Wake up, Mama. Wake up!" She started shaking her mother as she tried to get her to open her eyes. She could barely hear the whispers of the crowd wondering where her father was, and people sharing that he was never around. A hand touched her shoulder.

"I'm sorry child, but we need to go," someone said. Cress pushed the hand off her shoulder and continued to try to wake her mother. Then a pair of hands reached down and picked her up off the ground. She tried desperately to pull out of their grasp, but the hands were too strong. Then as if a dam broke, her knees buckled, and tears fell down her face as she started wailing, leaning against the hands holding her up.

"Come on dear, we're going to go to the chapel." The hands that kept her from falling picked her up and started carrying her away from her mother and her home.

It turned out that one of the chapel servants had been around when the doctor had told her that her mother was dead. Cress had become numb and unaware of her surroundings until she was set down in front of the chapel doors. That's when she looked up at the woman in the yellow dress that people who served in the chapels wore.

"We're going to go inside and head on into the kitchens to get you something warm to eat, alright?" the woman said, kneeling down to Cress's level.

Cress barely nodded her head. The woman got up and started walking. Cress followed behind. After going through the chapel doors, Cress was led toward the kitchen. There weren't that many people there, but there was stew cooking over the fire. The chapel servant grabbed a bowl from the cupboard and ladled some of the stew into it. She set the bowl in front of Cress, who hardly ate any of it.

After a while, the chapel servant took the mostly filled bowl away and gently placed her hand on Cress's shoulder. "Do you want to go to sleep now?"

Again, Cress only nodded and followed the woman out of the kitchen, past the sanctuary, and into a hallway filled with doors.

"These are all of the rooms where guests in need of sanctuary stay. You can have this room to yourself. Lavatories are across the hall from the rooms," the chapel servant said and opened up a door to a small room. It had a small bed, a wash basin, and a trunk where clothes and other personal items could go. Cress walked into the room and looked out the window. She saw that it looked out onto the chapel's gardens, with part of the kitchen garden closest to her room.

"Right, well, if you need anything, you can find me in the kitchen," the woman said and then closed the door after she left, leaving Cress alone for the first time since she had learned about her mother's death.

When Cress had first started looking out the window, the sun was still high up in the sky, but when she finally walked away to her new bed, the sun had long since set. She sat on the bed, tucked her knees up under her chin, and started sobbing.

It was only a short time later that her door opened up. Cress looked up and tried to wipe the tears from her face, but most of them had dried on her cheeks.

A mop of black hair was the first thing she saw through the crack in her door. "*Psst.* You awake?"

"Weasel?" she whispered.

"Is that what you call me?" the boy asked as he fully walked in.

"Sorry, I never actually learned your name."

Weasel grinned, and for some reason she fixated on the fact that at some point during the day, he had lost another tooth.

"I like it. Now come on. We have to go." He tugged on her hand to get her off her bed.

"Wait, where are we going?"

Weasel sighed as he rubbed the back of his neck. "I owe you one."

It didn't answer her question, but Cress decided that it didn't really matter where he took her. Whether she went with him or stayed at the chapel, she no longer truly belonged anywhere.

The two children crept out of Cress's room and made their way quietly through the chapel. Cress had stopped paying attention to where Weasel was going. She just continued to let him guide her by holding her hand.

"We're here."

Cress finally took in her surroundings and gasped when she saw her mother's shop. It had been boarded up in the short time that she had been taken to the chapel and then led back here. She turned and looked at Weasel who was eyeing the outside stairs that led to the living quarters. "Why did you bring me here?"

Instead of answering her, the urchin boy walked up the stairs and stopped in front of the door.

"It's locked," Cress told him.

Still not saying a word, Weasel pulled out a thin metal rod and started to pick the lock. The door opened easily as he finished.

"No one lets children like us get our stuff before we have to leave." Weasel looked down and lightly kicked the floor.

Cress could feel tears fill her eyes as she took one last walk through her childhood home. There wasn't much even worth keeping, but after some thought, she went to the little chair next to the fireplace. Her sewing basket was right where she had left it the night before. Picking it up tenderly, she snuggled her face into the cloth that she had practiced her embroidery on and let her tears fall soundlessly into the folds.

She looked over at Weasel and whispered in a hoarse voice, "Thank you."

He nodded in acknowledgement and waited for her to finish up before taking her back to the chapel.

CHAPTER 18

It started raining just as Garrett walked out from under the canopy.

"Perfect," he muttered.

He stomped toward the lake edge despite being soaked to the bone. How could Cress possibly think that some ball gown was more important than their life? He needed this curse broken as soon as possible; didn't she understand that? For a brief moment he considered testing the limits of the curse, trying to figure out a way to break it on his own without her.

"Argh!" Garrett grasped his chest and doubled over. A sharp, shooting pain pierced his heart.

"Alright, I'm not going to leave her," he gasped. Immediately, the pain went away, but exhaustion filled its place, bringing Garrett to his knees. Tears mixed with the rain as both flowed down his face.

Garrett had never before felt such a loss of control as he did now. When he had lived out on the streets, he was able to look out for himself, join the military, and provide for himself. Even after his failed attempt at becoming King of Lyra, he still managed to land on his feet. He also knew how to fix his mistakes, even if it took a while.

But this time, he had to rely on someone else, and he resented it.

"Hoseenu, don't you think I've suffered enough?" he croaked out.

When no answer came, he finally got up and went back to the tent. Cress put out the fire before she went to sleep, so he stripped off his wet clothes and heaped them into a pile, not caring that they wouldn't dry that way. He would never admit it to Cress, but he also loathed the "swan clothes" as they called them. The clothes always disappeared when they turned back into swans. They also discovered that whatever they changed into the night before, those items seemed to transform into the swan clothes. Cress always made sure to change back into the white feathered dress before dawn, so she wouldn't have to worry about it. Garrett tried to not change into anything else if he could help it so he wouldn't have that problem.

Garrett blindly reached into the tent where they kept a pile of towels for drying off in case they transformed into humans while still out on the water. He wrapped himself in the towel and went to his bed mat. He glanced at Cress's side of the tent to see if she was asleep. Her back was to him, and from her uneven breathing he could tell that she was still awake.

He opened his mouth but realized that he didn't actually have anything to say to her, so he lay down and pulled the blankets over his head.

Cress heard Garrett come in, but she didn't think she could face him. He was Weasel, and he remembered her. While she never thought that she would forget the boy who had teased her but later helped her retrieve her sewing basket, she apparently had. Now she was cursed, stuck with him.

Hoseenu, how did this happen? she had prayed as she finally started working on Sophia's dress. She could see Garrett kneeling near the lake, but she didn't think he wanted her around. So she did what she knew best: sewed dresses.

Then, like a coward, she stuffed everything away, put out the dwindling embers, and rushed to bed as soon as she saw him get up. He seemed to have assumed she was asleep because he didn't say his customary goodnight.

She lay awake hoping that she would fall asleep at some point. Garrett's breathing had evened out in slumber hours ago, and the rain had stopped pattering the roof of the tent shortly afterwards.

Slowly, Cress got up and snuck out through the tent flap. The sky was still covered with clouds, but a light breeze seemed to be pushing them away as dawn started to appear. The air smelled of fresh rain, and Cress was miserable.

"You should be a swan."

Cress jumped at the feminine voice that came from the tree line. The witch glared at her with her arms crossed over her chest.

"Life is full of surprises, isn't it?" Cress shrugged while she tried to slow down her heartbeat.

The witch left the edge of the clearing and came to stand right in front her. Again Cress found herself looking up at someone, and this time it was even more unpleasant.

"What are you doing here?"

The witch smirked, "I don't think we've been properly introduced. I'm Willow," The redheaded woman waited for Cress to acknowledge her, but Cress stayed quiet.

"I was looking for a dead swan," Willow sniffed after she gave up on Cress speaking.

Cress gaped at her, "What do you mean a dead swan? Garrett's alive."

"So it would seem. No matter how you managed to remain a human right now, I was still able to feel my curse starting to kill him. I wanted to witness my handiwork."

"That's impossible. I didn't attempt to leave him, and I'm not dying."

Willow's smile caused her nose to scrunch up. "You must not be worth sticking around for then." But then she frowned, continuing, "Or at least the beginning pain of a broken heart was enough for him to stay with you. Oh well, maybe I'll luck out next time."

"There won't be a next time."

Both Willow and Cress turned to where Garrett stood, covered in just a towel. Cress's face heated up and she was sure that it had turned bright red as she quickly looked away. Willow, on the other hand, blatantly looked him up and down.

"I might have made a mistake turning you into a swan," she purred.

"Leave. Now," Garrett said through gritted teeth.

"Fine. But I'll be back to check on you, my pet." Again, the witch disappeared into thin air.

"Garrett, I'm –"

"Not now Cress," Garrett said wearily. "I'm going to try to sleep for a little bit longer. You probably should too."

Cress watched as Garrett went back inside, but wasn't sure if she could sleep. She looked over to the east and saw that the dawn light had gotten brighter, the sun just about to peek over the horizon.

Throwing her shoulders back, she waltzed up to the tent and stepped into the path of the tent flap right at the moment the sun officially showed itself. She could hear a human groan from underneath the blankets on Garrett's bed mat right before a swan's head poked out. He blinked when he saw her standing in the doorway, the tent flap resting on her feathered body.

"I can let it close if you want to be trapped in the tent all day."

They had discovered one day that once the tent's flap closed during the day, it was enchanted to stay shut while they were swans. It was nice of Tatiana to include that to protect their items from damage or being stolen, but they had unfortunately discovered that they couldn't leave when they turned into swans inside the tent. Cress would have blushed if she could when she remembered all the cleaning they had had to do when they finally turned human for the night.

"Uh, no. I don't want to be trapped." Garrett got completely out from under his blankets and stepped outside while Cress held the flap open.

As soon as he was completely outside, Cress let the tent seal itself shut for the day. She heard Garrett's intake of breath as his beak opened, but she interrupted, saying, "I'm going to go flying to clear my head," and left him standing there.

CHAPTER 19

He almost died. Cress was flying over the Elven Wood but couldn't admire the view like she usually did when she was up in the air. Garrett had almost left her after they had argued about her working on Sophia's dress rather than working to break the curse.

Cress flapped her wings once to keep herself up on the air current. If she were human, she knew that she would be crying. A dress wasn't worth a life, and that's almost how it turned out. At the same time though, it wasn't as if she could let Sophia not have something to wear to an important ball. If Garrett just stuck around and waited, then she wouldn't have to worry about him.

Hoseenu, help me. Please.

Instead of divine intervention, an arrow whizzed

past her, almost hitting her wing. She squawked and started to circle overhead to see if she could find where the arrow had come from. A burly man holding a bow was looking up toward the sky with his hand shielding his eyes from the glaring sun.

There was a hunter in the Elven Wood.

As soon as Cress's beak was aimed back toward the lake, she stopped her circle and flew straight.

"Garrett!" She cried out as she landed on the water. She saw him near the tall cattails that could easily hide them.

He rushed toward her. "Cress, what is it?"

"There's a hunter. We have to hide!" Without thinking, she gently pressed the side of her head to Garrett's as she tried to calm herself down.

She felt him press back before he said, "Which direction did he come from?"

"I don't know. West maybe?"

"Ok, see the lake weed over there?" Garrett nodded toward the tall grass-looking plants growing out of the water near the edge.

"Yes."

"We're going to swim into it and then keep our heads down. Sunset is just a couple of hours away and then we won't be prey anymore."

Cress followed him as he floated on top of the water and into the tall lake weed. As soon as they were nestled inside, they laid their necks down over their bodies.

A couple of hours passed and Cress didn't dare say a word the whole time. She was thankful that she hadn't, because right as she was starting to feel her body relax, a rustling came from the far side of the lake. She saw Garrett position himself to peek through the lake weed to see what had made the noise.

"What is it?" she whispered, but he just shook his head, so she didn't say another word.

After what felt like hours, Garrett slowly raised his head and she followed suit.

"He's gone."

"What did he look like?" she asked.

"Hefty but short. He had a few ducks stringed up laying across his horse's saddle."

Cress shivered. That was too close. "No one is supposed to hunt in these woods. Do you think we should let someone know?"

"How? We didn't schedule anyone to check in on us, and if the elves are nearby, they're not going to show themselves to a pair of humans."

"Even a pair of humans who spend their days as swans?" Cress tried to put humor into her words, but it fell flat.

Instead of saying anything, Garrett swam toward the land. Cress sighed as she followed.

The sun set shortly after they set their webbed feet on dry ground.

Garrett was walking in front of Cress, and she felt the need to clear the tension between them.

"Garrett, I'm sorry about last night. I shouldn't have thrown your past in your face like that, and maybe you don't think so, but I really don't want this curse to kill you. Let's start working on the shirts now."

He finally stopped walking, but she was still talking

to his back. His shoulders dropped right before he turned around.

"And I ended up moving into the castle shortly afterwards, so I can't remember if I ever thanked you, but thank you for helping me get my mother's sewing basket."

Garrett smiled for the first time since she taught him how to knit with his hands. "Who would have thought that this weasel would turn out to be a swan."

Cress choked back a sob as she ran up to him and squeezed him tightly. "Don't you dare die on me out here. I still have a decent aim, and I will throw mud at you if you do!"

She could feel his laughter rumbling in his chest as he returned her hug.

"I'll keep that in mind." He pulled back but stayed in her embrace. "I don't know about you, but I didn't get a lot of sleep and I feel like I'm going to fall asleep standing right here."

Cress pulled back and tried to discreetly wipe away the tears from her eyes. "I could use some sleep too."

Garrett grinned, "We should also try to find the hunter tomorrow morning before we turn back."

"You think that's a good idea?"

He nodded, "I'd rather know if he was here for just the day or if he is actually camping out in the woods."

"Alright, but tomorrow night we are going to work on breaking this curse." She pointed her finger at him and glared, which made him laugh again.

He held up his hands in surrender. "As you wish, m'lady."

"I do wish," she said haughtily before cracking a smile.

They walked into their tent and quickly let their exhaustion claim them.

CHAPTER 20

Garrett stared up at the tent ceiling and listened to Cress breathing. It was one of the most soothing sounds he had ever heard: another human being feeling safe enough in his presence to let their guard down. He grew up alone on the streets. Even when he stayed at the chapel on cold nights, the chapel servants would give him a whole room to himself. At the military bases, everyone shared rooms, but with people on opposite shifts so that there were beds for everyone. He was used to being alone. He would enjoy being in another's presence, even though she didn't really have much of a choice in the matter.

Stretching where he lay, he felt his back pop. He moved the blankets off of himself, trying to be as quiet as possible. Apparently it wasn't quiet enough; Cress started to shift in her sleep which he had learned meant that she was about to wake up. Giving up the idea that he could let her sleep longer, he stood up without any hesitancy and exited the tent. The moon was full, which he thanked Hoseenu for, because that would make finding the hunter's trail a lot easier between now and when the sun rose in a couple of hours.

He felt a huge smile on his face when he heard the tent flap open behind him.

"Morning."

Cress shambled next to him with her eyes closed and mumbled something.

"What was that?" He bent down so he could hear her better.

"Morning," she yawned with her eyes still closed.

Her long blond hair was still a rat's nest, and there were crease lines up and down her right cheek. He thought she had never looked more beautiful. "Come on Sunshine, we need to go to the other side of the lake."

Cress blinked a couple of times as she slapped her cheeks. "I'm ready when you are."

He just snickered and started walking, Cress keeping pace beside him.

It wasn't long after they got to the where he had last seen the hunter when Garrett picked up the man's trail. Honestly, he was a little disappointed by how easy it was to see which direction the hunter went. The ducks that he had seen must have been unlucky, because there was no way that any animal wouldn't have been able to hear the man coming based on all of the broken branches and plants that littered his trail.

"Why don't you look happy? Are you not able to find his trail?"

Garrett turned to look at Cress. "What do you mean?"

"You've been frowning this whole time."

"Actually, he's going to be really easy to follow. I feel like I'm wasting all of my military training tracking him." He showed off a crooked grin and barked out a laugh when Cress rolled her eyes.

"I'm so sorry that our hunt is going so easily for you. If you want, I can walk all over his footprints and whatever else you trackers need to follow your quarry." She tried to give him a deadpan look, but he saw the mischief in her eyes.

"Actually, would you be so kind as to do that for me?" Without thinking he wrapped an arm around her shoulders and pulled her closer to him. But when she let out a small squeak, he quickly dropped his arm and muttered, "Sorry."

They didn't say anything else while he led them down the trail that the hunter had ended up taking. It wasn't until he stopped abruptly that Cress whispered, "What is it?"

He frowned. "I think I hear voices up ahead. I'm going to try to find us a way through the trees so we won't be seen by anyone that's further up the path."

Cress nodded and they slowly moved off of the trail and into the thick woods. Garrett tried to guide them carefully, stepping on ground that wasn't covered in dead underbrush so that no one would hear them approaching.

By this point, dawn was imminent, making everything around them brighter. Garrett wished that they could have changed out of their white clothes before leaving, but he hadn't wanted to risk losing any dark clothing when they inevitably changed into swans away from the tent.

It wasn't long before he spotted the man from earlier talking with someone else. Garrett couldn't tell who because the man was blocking his view. He motioned for Cress to squat next to him behind some bushes when they got close enough to hear what they were saying.

"You want me to catch *how much*?" the hunter said to his companion.

"Enough to feed one hundred men."

"And where are these hundred men? I can't keep hunting for you and your friend if you're just selling the meat at a higher price."

The hunter had just stepped back and gave Garrett a full view of the other man's face. Garrett hissed under his breath.

"What is it?" Cress mouthed.

"It's one of the leaders of the raiders. We must be close to where they're hiding if he's trying to get food around here."

Cress only nodded, but he saw that she was frowning. Before he could ask her what she was thinking, he saw that the sun had just come up over the horizon and they were swans again. Cress gasped and he checked to see if she was alright, but then she bobbed her head toward where the two men were standing. Garrett turned his head back and exhaled sharply.

Where once there were trees behind the two talking men, a field had appeared filled with tents and people going about their morning business.

"We found their hideout, but why can we see it now?" Cress whispered.

"I...I don't know." Garrett was waiting for the hunter to comment on what they were seeing, but he seemed unphased.

Instead, the hunter was saying, "If I find out that you're cheating me out of good money, I'll no longer be doing business with you."

"That wouldn't be a good idea. You wouldn't want us to have to report that the source came from Elven territory, now, would you?"

The hunter blanched as he stumbled around for words. "It's not like you could prove it."

"The animals in these woods are the best quality. Everyone knows this and anyone can clearly see the difference between ones raised near elves versus those near humans." The raider smiled down at the shorter man.

"Fine, I best be off to find some game," the hunter said and stalked off.

The raider watched for a moment and then turned around and went to the main part of the camp.

"Do you think we can see it because we're no longer human?" Cress asked Garrett after they were sure the hunter was truly gone.

"It's possible. Regardless, we really need to get out of here."

They both slowly waddled backwards and tried to make as little noise as possible as they went back toward the part of the trail that was out of sight of the raiders' camp. As soon as they arrived, Garrett raised his wings and looked over at Cress to see that she had caught on to his signal to fly back to the tent. Then they took off and flew back to their temporary home.

CHAPTER 21

The water was cold when Cress landed. She bristled a little bit and felt her tail wiggle to shake off the droplets that had sprayed onto her. The sound of another splash came from behind her as Garrett also landed.

"We have to tell someone," Cress told him.

She watched as Garrett shook off the water that had gotten on him. "Agreed, but it's still not safe to fly to the castle from here."

"We'll just have to risk it."

Garrett didn't say anything for a while. "How did Tatiana know to come when we were first cursed? It wasn't made very clear to me."

"She said that morning to ask Hoseenu to send her if I were to get into trouble, or something along those lines."

"Do you think that we could do that now?" he wondered.

"Maybe? Tatiana isn't my fairy godmother though. Hoseenu might have her off doing something else," she huffed.

Softly, Garrett said, "That doesn't change the fact that Hoseenu still cares and listens to us."

Cress had been swimming in circles while trying to figure out their next move, but when he spoke, she stopped so she could face him. "True...since when did you actually start trusting that Hoseenu cares?"

He ducked his head. "After I left Lyra to track down the raiders."

Cress waited for him to continue, letting the silence drag out, and was rewarded when he started squirming before he said, "You knew I was being blackmailed, but only Liam knows the full reason why."

Cress couldn't help but snort, "Liam? The man who probably hated you more than I used to? That Liam?"

Garrett's beak opened slightly in what Cress referred to as the swan grin. "Yes, that Liam. Wait, used to hate me?"

She quickly looked the other way. "Don't change the subject."

He stared at her for a moment, but then continued. "To be fair, he was slightly terrifying when he was more beast than man, so it was in my best interest to share what he wanted to know." He paused to take a deep breath. "Which was that I was being blackmailed because someone knew that when I was patrolling the border, I was paid to look the other way when the raiders were sneaking around doing whatever business they had planned during my shift."

"Is that how you knew the man from today?"

He tilted his head to look at her, "That's what you're focusing on? Not that I betrayed my country's trust, and not that this is just another example of why you should think the worst of me?"

Cress lifted her wings as if to shrug. "We're talking about how you came to trust Hoseenu so deeply."

Honestly, Cress didn't want to say that she wasn't all that surprised. It wasn't hard to figure out that he and the raiders had had some sort of arrangement. It was just a matter of details. Plus, she was tired of being mad at him. When she found out that he had almost died because he thought about leaving her after she kept bringing up his past mistakes, she realized that she never wanted to make a person feel that way again.

Garrett continued, "Anyway, I decided I needed to make everything right by finding out where the raiders were hiding. While I was out searching, I had too much time by myself and I started remembering what the chapel servants had taught us as kids. That Hoseenu made everything and everyone. That he loves us and all that stuff. Then one day while I was following a lead, my horse tossed a shoe and started limping. There wasn't any blacksmith for miles around, and I couldn't find the horseshoe to try to put it back on myself. That's when a man came traveling down the same road in the opposite direction and asked if I needed a hand. For some reason he had an extra horseshoe in his saddlebag that would fit my horse's hoof perfectly.

"While he was applying the horseshoe, we started talking. He kept talking about how he went wherever Hoseenu told him to go, and that day he knew that he was supposed to bring a horseshoe with him and ride this path. When he finished with my horse, he told me, 'Son, Hoseenu loves you.' And then he disappeared. It was then that I actually believed everything that the chapel servants taught us."

A warmth spread throughout Cress's body as Garrett shared his story. She knew that Hoseenu cared, but it always made her happy whenever she took the time to actually remember.

"What about you?"

Garrett's voice brought Cress out of her musings. "Hmm?"

"When did you actually believe that Hoseenu didn't just look out for royalty or important people?"

"I think it was when He sent Tatiana to the chapel to bring me to the castle. One night I asked Him if He actually loved me like the chapel servants said He did. It had been hard losing my mother and not knowing what would happen to me. The next morning, I woke up to find that a fairy godmother had come to bring me to the castle. It was just for a mending position underneath the castle tailor, but I'm pretty sure it was Tatiana who made sure that Ravenna and I met, and Ravenna practically became my sister. Tatiana never actually said it, but I'm almost certain that Hoseenu told her to come get me because He knew I just needed proof in that moment that He listens to me."

"It's true," they heard from across the lake.

Both Cress and Garrett let out a honk and flapped their wings, but calmed down as soon as they saw Tatiana on the lake shore.

"Tatiana!" Cress eagerly swam up to her. Garrett followed, not far behind her.

"Hello, love. Are you alright?" She chuckled. "All things considered that is."

"We discovered something, and we need to tell Sophia right away," Cress told her.

"It's a good thing then that I brought a couple of horses with me this time."

Cress peered behind the fairy godmother and saw that there were two horses standing next to the tent.

"As soon as the sun sets, we can leave, but until then, how about you fill me in."

The two swans started telling their story. Tatiana looked progressively more and more concerned as she listened.

"I think Willow's magic is how they are able to hide their camp," Garrett finished off.

"It would seem so," Tatiana agreed. "How far along are you with your shirts?"

Cress and Garrett looked at each other, then Cress bowed her head. "We only just finished gathering all of the nettles we think we'll need."

Tatiana pursed her lips. "You're only able to turn human as long as you're close to the lake at sunset. I wasn't strong enough to alter Willow's magic to allow you to transform into humans outside this vicinity."

"We can stay here, and as soon as we're done, we'll take the horses back to the castle. Besides, humans, and I'm guessing probably fairies, won't be able to see through the veil. You'll need us as swans to help guide the way so that when Sophia's ready, she can send soldiers to take care of the raiders," Garrett offered.

"That would explain why He said to bring horses," Tatiana muttered to herself. Straightening up, she said to the swans, "Alright. I don't like how close you are to danger, but it is what it is. I'll let Sophia know what you've discovered, and I'm sure that as soon as she finds out, she'll want to have someone come with you, so they know exactly what we're dealing with."

"Wait! Can you bring Sophia's dress back with you?"

Before Tatiana could reply, Garrett spoke up. "When did you finish?"

"Um. A couple of nights ago," Cress sheepishly left it at that, not wanting to bring up how it was actually right after they had fought.

"Oh. Right."

Tatiana looked between the two but didn't comment. Instead, she said, "I can do that. Please be safe." Then she bent down and kissed the top of Cress's head. "Ravenna's arriving next week. I thought you should be prepared."

"What?! She can't!" Cress squawked, but Tatiana had disappeared.

"What's wrong?" Garrett asked.

"Ravenna isn't supposed to know about this! She's already got so much going on that she doesn't need this too."

"But you said that you two are basically sisters, wouldn't she want to know?"

Cress groaned, "Yes, but that doesn't negate the fact that she is a queen and a busy one at that. Come on, we need to finish those shirts." She started waddling out of the water and toward the tent.

"Cress?"

She turned to look back at Garrett. "Yes?"

"It's only midday," he chuckled.

Sure enough, the sun was shining bright in the middle of the sky. Nowhere near the western horizon. Cress heaved a sigh. "Fine. I guess the shirts can wait until we have actual hands."

Garrett continued to laugh.

CHAPTER 22

The leaves of the woods rustled, signaling the movement of the many nocturnal animals that lived there. Garrett was thankful that he and Cress didn't remain prey animals while the predators were awake and hunting. He set down the body of his half-finished shirt so that he could give his hands a break. Get-ting up, he reached around the stump he was sitting on so he could grab the salve they had made for the night.

Rubbing it over his burning hands, he watched as Cress concentrated on the nettles in her lap, her hands deftly twisting and turning to create elegant stitches. His stitches made him hope that for Cress's sake, the curse would be broken based on the fact that it was *technically* a shirt, but nothing like the *actual* shirt that Cress was making.

The dressmaker looked up and caught him watching her. He gave her the lopsided grin that for some reason always caused her to narrow her eyes at him.

"Looks like we're going to be done for the night." She nodded her head at the salve in his hands.

He handed the rest to her after she put her shirt down. "Did you ever think that you would ever be thankful to not have hands to feel during the day?"

"No. I never did. It's nice to know though that stinging nettles don't bother feathers."

They had been able to work on the shirts for a few days now, but despite Cress's determination that they were going to finish them as soon as possible, they had quickly discovered that they were limited to touching the nettles for only a short period of time each night. They had agreed that as soon as one of them needed the salve to stop the pain from becoming too unbearable, they would both stop for the night.

"When do you think someone will be out here to check up on the raiders?" she asked him when she was done soothing her hands.

"I would have thought the day after we told Tatiana, but I guess not. Are you worried that something will happen to us out here?"

"I am a little worried, but we've been here for a couple of weeks now and we had no idea that they were even close enough to be concerned about. I'm more worried about the lack of elves."

It was strange that they were in elven territory and there had been no sign of them. Especially if the raiders felt comfortable hiding out in their woods.

"I also wonder if everything is okay with them," he

agreed. "Even though they keep to themselves, they would have at least investigated two humans who turn into swans at the edge of their territory.

Standing up, he stretched his stiff muscles. He didn't know how Cress could make a career out of something that involved so much of sitting. "Do you want to go for a walk?"

She threw her head back in surprise. "Right now? In the middle of the night?"

"Yeah, why not?"

"For several reasons. Mainly so we can get some rest." She stood up. "But it might be nice to do something out of routine for a change." They put away the nettles and the shirts before tending to the horses. Tatiana seemed to have made an invisible barrier for the animals, because while Cress and Garrett were swans, the horses were able to roam free, but they never left the area around the lake and their little clearing. At night, the newly-turned humans would brush them down and make sure they were alright, occasionally riding them around the woods so they could get more exercise. They would then repeat the grooming routine as soon as they finished knitting for the night.

Once the horses had been groomed, Cress and Garrett started walking along the path that circled the lake. The moon was starting its half-full phase, so they were not only able to see where they were going, but also more of the stars in the sky.

They had been walking for a while when Garrett said, "You haven't mentioned if you're being courted by anyone."

Cress stopped in her tracks, but Garrett continued walking. He didn't want her to see the sweat on his face from how vulnerable he felt.

"Why would you ask me that now?" she asked when she caught up to him.

He shrugged. "We have been pretty busy since meeting up at the Wilderosian capital. We haven't really had the time to talk about it."

"I haven't mentioned being courted because I'm not," She nonchalantly tried to brush it off. Obviously uncomfortable talking about not having anyone to be with. "What about you? Are you courting any woman?"

He just turned his head to look at her, eyebrow raised.

"Right. I guess Willow would technically be the last woman you had dealings with."

As they continued walking, they fell into an awkward silence. Garrett cursed himself for bringing up whether or not there was another man in her life. It's not like it should matter to him if there was. Although a part of him felt like insisting that she was his mate, he tried to brush that off as something caused by the curse.

When they had completed the circuit around the lake, he stopped to look at the moon's reflection on the water. He didn't expect Cress to join him after he made things so uncomfortable, but she stayed by his side until they were both ready to go to sleep.

CHAPTER 23

"Cress, I need you to come out here right now." Cress's eyes shot wide open. She knew that voice. She would recognize that voice no matter how long she went without hearing it. Ravenna was here.

She quickly sat up and saw that Garrett was already awake and out of the tent as predawn light filtered in. She rubbed her face, remembering Garrett's topic of conversation from the night before. Why would he ask her if she had a man in her life? When would she have had the time between focusing on her career, traveling to Wilderose, and getting cursed into a swan to even think about letting someone into the mess that was her life? She never seemed to have time to consider courtship. Besides, she had Ravenna to spend time with whenever she was not working. But now that Ravenna was married, Cress wanted her friend to have time with Liam. It just had also made her realize how alone she felt outside of designing dresses.

Well, if she was going to be honest with herself, the swan-man was growing on her. But she wasn't planning on being honest with herself, at least not yet. She was planning on figuring out who told Ravenna where she was located and teaching them a lesson about keeping a secret.

Deciding she had stalled enough, she walked out of the tent and then immediately thought about walking back inside. Not only was Ravenna present, but so were Liam, Sophia, her entire personal guard, and Tatiana. Garrett stood off to the side with his arms crossed talking with Liam. Cress snickered at the sight of the two men scowling at each other.

When Ravenna saw that Cress had inally emerged from the tent, she rushed over and hugged Cress tight. "Why in Hoseenu's name did I just ind out last night that my best friend has been cursed for the better part of a month?"

Tears pricked Cress's eyes as she hugged her friend back. "I didn't want you to worry."

Ravenna stepped back and looked up at Cress. After standing next to only Garrett for the past month, it was weird for Cress to remember that she was actually taller than a lot of people. Ravenna especially.

"Well, I was going to worry about it no matter what. This better not happen again."

Cress laughed, "Alright, alright. I'll make sure that whenever I get cursed next, I'll tell you right away."

Ravenna glared at her. "When I said, 'not happen again,' I also meant getting cursed." But then she cracked a smile. "I've missed you."

"I've missed you too."

In the next moment, Cress went from looking down at Ravenna to looking up.

"Oh. The both of you really do turn into swans," was all Ravenna said.

Cress turned and saw Garrett and Liam walking toward the two women, followed by Sophia and Tatiana. Garrett waddled to stand next to Cress and she had to do everything in her power to not greet him by pressing her head to his.

"Why did you think we didn't?" Cress asked Ravenna. "You were human until just a few seconds ago, so it didn't really sink in."

"Wait, you can talk while you're swans?!" Liam exclaimed. He turned to glare at Tatiana. "How are they able to talk when they turn into animals, but I couldn't when I was a dog?"

Cress saw Ravenna hiding a laugh behind her hand while Tatiana shrugged, "The witch who initially cursed them wasn't particularly thorough."

Liam just grumbled to himself and Ravenna stopped hiding her laughter. Liam smiled and pulled Ravenna to his side to hug her and said, "It was worth it since I got to marry you." He kissed the top of her head. Ravenna was smiling so big as she looked lovingly up at her husband and king.

Cress's beak opened into a smile of her own. It was so good to see her friend happy after all the heartache she had been through. Cress longedfor someone to love her as well. Shaking her head as if she could shake the thought away, she said, "I hate to interrupt, but we do have a real problem that doesn't involve being a swan."

"Right, Tatiana said that you found where the raiders are located," Sophia pitched in.

Garrett nodded. "It seems like they've been hiding at least a hundred people within the outer Elven Wood. They also hired a witch so that no human can see their encampment."

"Does that mean Tatiana can see them?" Ravenna asked.

"We can find out, but I would guess that they know that I'm as much of a threat, if not more so, than any human. They would have to be extremely foolish to not hide themselves from fairy godmothers as well." Tatiana said.

"Let's test it out then. Garrett, can you lead me and Tatiana to their location? Or at least a place where we can observe without them spotting us." Liam looked down at Garrett.

It seemed that no matter how much they despised the other's company, they did work well together when they were on a mission.

"I can. It'll take a few hours to get there though," Garrett answered.

"Then let's head out now."

"I'm going with you." Sophia stepped closer to her brother and grabbed his arm to stop him.

"Soph, I can't let you come. It's too dangerous," Liam pleaded with his sister.

"As Queen of Wilderose, this is part of my responsibility. I also want to see if we run into any of our elf friends. It's not like the elves to ignore humans camping within their borders."

Liam's shoulders dropped in resignation. "Fine. You can come with us." He turned to his wife. "Can you and Cress stay here with the guards? Please?" His eyes pleaded with her.

"She and I weren't done catching up, so I was planning on it." Ravenna raised her brow at Cress, which Cress knew meant they were going to be catching up on more than just Ravenna's and Liam's honeymoon.

"Great. Now, let's go."

Liam, Sophia, and Tatiana walked toward the horses, but Garrett stayed back for a moment.

"Please be safe while I'm gone," he said as he pressed his head to Cress's. The butterflies in her chest fluttered furiously, which made her feel a little sick.

"Of course I will. When have I not?" she teased.

Garrett rolled his eyes. "When you stepped in between me and a witch. When a hunter shot an arrow at you. I can go on, if you'd like."

Cress caught sight of Ravenna's eyes widening, so Cress quickly said, "No, that's alright. You need to get going." She shoved him forward with her head, making him chuckle.

Ravenna and Cress watched as their friends got onto their horses and Garrett took off into the air. Ravenna waved goodbye, but Cress could only lift one of her wings in a salute. As soon as they were out of sight, Ravenna turned to Cress.

"You have a lot of explaining to do."

"I don't know what you mean." Cress looked everywhere but at Ravenna. The lake, the grass, the tent...as long as her friend wasn't in its view, she was looking at it.

"First, you stepped in front of Garrett to protect him from a witch? Second, you're both cursed together.

Third, what did he mean by a hunter shooting an arrow at you?" Ravenna ticked off each item on her hand.

"It's kind of a long story."

"We've got time." Ravenna crossed her arms over her chest. Seeing as how there wasn't any way to get out of telling Ravenna, Cress started at the beginning when she had first run into Garrett in the marketplace.

The two friends moved to the fire pit so Ravenna could sit on one of the stumps, and Cress nested in front of her. By the time Cress had finished telling her story, Ravenna slowly shook her head. "I can't believe that Garrett's life is tied to yours."

Cress winced. "I know. It scares me to think that a person could die because of me."

"I'm really sorry, Cress, that you've had to go through this alone." Ravenna tilted her head. "Well, not alone exactly, but without your usual support system."

Cress lifted her shoulders in a shrug. "It's ok. Garrett actually hasn't been that bad to be around."

Ravenna gave Cress a conspiratorial smile. "He is pretty sweet when he wants to be, isn't he?" she trailed off.

"What are you implying?"

"Oh, just that even though what happened between me and Garrett ended up being a shame, that doesn't mean he's all bad." The Queen of Lyra tried her best to look innocent, but Cress saw right through her.

"Ravenna, it doesn't matter that he can be sweet or is 'not all that bad,' he broke your heart."

"And Hoseenu healed it and let Liam into my life," Ravenna retorted. "I've already had to do the work to forgive Garrett for what he did. His actions weren't right, but I've moved on. After you, Garrett, Liam, and I worked together solving the mystery behind those accidents, I realized that Garrett being around no longer bothered me. If anything, his presence bothers Liam more than it ever did me."

Ravenna got off her stump so that she could kneel in front of Cress. "I don't want to pressure you into anything, but I also want to make sure you're not using me as an excuse. I saw how he looked at you, and I know you well enough to know that nothing flusters you more than when you're interested in someone. In fact, it's really the only time you get flustered. Which isn't fair if you think about it." Ravenna put her hands on her hips and glared at Cress.

Cress laughed, "Well, I am awesome, so why should I get flustered?"

Ravenna looked up at the sky. "Hoseenu, help me to not strangle my best friend," she said before she also started cracking up.

Thankfully they switched to other topics, but Cress kept thinking back to what Ravenna had said about Cress being interested in Garrett. It wasn't possible! She was smart enough to know better than to fall for someone like him. She ignored the fact that Hoseenu seemed to have done a lot of work to soften Garrett. Cress decided to stop thinking about it while they were still cursed and just focus on being with her friend.

CHAPTER 24

Garrett landed softly on the road near his companions. Flying was still thrilling for him, and several times during their trip, he had to remember to not get caught up in the moment and make sure that he was still within sight of those on the ground so they could follow him. It took away some of the joy of being in the air.

He made sure that they were still some distance away from the raiders' camp. Up in the sky, he could see several dozen men and women out in the open. Only Hoseenu knew how many were actually staying there.

"We'll need to tie up the horses here and walk the rest of the way." he informed the group.

"Walk?" Liam stared pointedly at Garrett's webbed feet.

Garrett's feathers bristled and he lifted his head

high, which still only came up to Liam's mid-torso. "I can keep up."

Liam raised a brow, but didn't comment anymore about it. Instead, he turned to his sister and said, "You should wait here and guard the horses."

Sophia crossed her arms over her chest. "We've already discussed that I wasn't going to be left behind. Nice try though."

Liam glanced at Tatiana who just shook her head. "Fine. But you can't blame me for trying to protect my sister, can you?" He smiled.

Sophia smiled back before standing on her tiptoes and ruffling his red hair, laughing, "No, I can't."

"We need to stay quiet," Garrett hissed at the two siblings, who straightened up immediately.

As Garrett led the two monarchs and fairy godmother, he couldn't help but ruminate over the situation. He was essentially responsible for preventing two countries' leaders from getting caught by a band of people who were known to commit regicide. And he was stuck as a useless bird. He prayed that they would all make it back to the lake safely.

When they made it to the last bend in the road before the campsite, Garrett guided his group off into the woods. Despite Garrett's earlier insistence that he could walk just fine, he had to stretch his neck close to the ground to make sure that he could see where his feet would land so as to not step on anything that would give them away. Thankfully, Liam was able to guide the humans' feet so they wouldn't make any noise.

"Do you see it?" Liam whispered when Garrett stopped them.

Garrett looked back at the members of his party and could see that just like when Cress and Garrett were human, they couldn't see what was right in front of them. Even Tatiana's eyes continued to search the tree line in front of them. She looked at Garrett.

"This witch must have made sure that her cloaking spell would hide it even from me."

He had been afraid of this.

A stone's throw away from where they hid, different men were walking around the camp. Several were coming in and out of the various tents while others were doing tasks such as cooking and tending to the horses.

"I can see all of them." Garrett finally answered Liam and he saw Liam's face turn grim.

Slowly, they crept back the way they came so they could talk freely a distance away.

When they were in the clear, Sophia broke the dismal silence "What do we do now?" She looked expectantly at Tatiana.

"I don't know. I'll have to ask Hoseenu what to do now." Tatiana turned to Garrett. "We should head back to the lake so at least while we wait for an answer, you and Cress can work on breaking the curse."

Garrett bobbed his head in an attempt at a nod. "I'll fly and meet you there. Unless you need me to guide you?"

Liam shook his head. "I was able to keep track of the route on the way here."

Garrett nodded again and flapped his wings to start his flight back to Cress.

Cress heard Garrett before she saw him. The beating of his wings made the air whoosh around him. Finally, he cleared the treeline and gracefully landed on the lake near the shore where she and Ravenna were waiting.

Ravenna stood up from where she was sitting next to Cress and peered towards the path that led in the direction where Garrett had come from. Cress followed close behind.

"Where are the others?" Ravenna asked.

"They're not far behind me."

"Was Tatiana able to see through the barrier?" Cress inquired.

Garrett shook his head.

Cress's stomach twisted up inside of her. She would be lying if she said that having the villains nearby didn't bother her. It seemed even more prudent to finish the nettle-shirts before they were discovered by their neighbors.

Garrett swam up to the shoreline and shambled out of the water. When he got close to Cress he pressed his head to hers. However, neither of them seemed to notice how close to the horizon the sun had been because they found themselves completely pressed up against each other's human bodies.

Cress felt Garrett's arms just starting to wrap around her when Ravenna cleared her throat. Garrett immediately dropped his arms and stepped back.

"I don't interrupt you when you're having a moment with Liam." Cress whipped around to glare at Ravenna. However, as soon as the words left her mouth they seemed to hang in the air. Ravenna gave a strangled laugh and Cress heard Garrett take a quick intake of breath. Her cheeks instantly became hot and she could not make herself look at him.

Thankfully, they were distracted by the sound of horses plodding. Liam, Sophia, and Tatiana had returned.

Cress watched as Ravenna practically ran towards her husband and jumped into his arms after he had dismounted his horse. Liam caught her and kissed her soundly on the mouth.

"Should we interrupt their moment?" Garrett whispered into Cress's ear.

She shivered slightly, but before she could answer him, Garrett had left to go and talk with Tatiana and Sophia.

Hoseenu, help me. Cress prayed before joining the others.

"We need to head back before anyone notices our large caravan." she overheard Liam tell the group as she walked up next to Ravenna.

"But we're so close to them now and we have two people who can see their location." Sophia argued back.

"That doesn't help us if our soldiers can't see the enemy even if we're lucky enough that the magic stops working past the barrier.. Tatiana said she needed time to figure out how we'd be able to see them before we attack," Ravenna answered. "Besides, I'd rather Cress and Garrett stay safe while they try to finish breaking their curse."

Cress reached over and squeezed Ravenna's hand and mouthed "Thank you" when Ravenna glanced over at her.

"You're right. I just wanted all of this behind us."

Sophia smiled at Cress. "But it would be awful for you two to get trapped near a battlefield while still working on becoming human again."

Cress smiled back, but she could feel anxiety tightening her chest as she thought about all of the work that she and Garrett still needed to do for their shirts. As much as she loved being able to visit with Ravenna and everyone else again, she wished that they would hurry and leave.

"Then it's settled." Liam spoke up after a moment of silence. "Since it's too late now, we'll pack up and leave in the morning."

Everyone else agreed and started to unpack the supplies that they had brought for this very case. While they did that, Cress went into hers and Garrett's tent to pull out her shirt. There wasn't much time left before the inevitable exhaustion hit after being awake all day with Ravenna, but she still wanted to make some progress. Any was better than none if it meant leaving the raiders far behind them sooner. However, she just wanted to go to sleep and wake up to everything being perfectly fine.

"You okay?" A familiar deep voice asked from behind her. She turned around and watched as Garrett entered the tent.

She gave him a wan smile. "Of course. Why wouldn't I be?"

In one stride Garrett walked over and sat next to her. "Because you haven't rested today. Because you've had a lot of human interaction after practically having none for a long time now." He tilted his head and raised an eyebrow as if to say "Should I go on?"

She heaved a sigh. "Alright, I am tired, but if you want the truth... "

"I always want the truth from you." Garrett quickly interrupted.

Cress continued, "I just want to return to normal life as soon as possible. I don't like feeling trapped on this lake and I think that's what's finally started to take a toll on me."

Garrett remained silent to the point where Cress started to wonder if he regretted telling her that he always wanted the truth, but then he finally spoke. "I feel the same way. It'd be nice to no longer have to worry about being eaten."

He smiled down at her and she could feel her heart flip. "Yeah, it'd be nice being closer to the top of the food chain." She quipped.

Reaching out his hand for her to take it, he said, "Come on, let's work on these shirts while everyone else is sleeping."

Without hesitation she placed her hand in his and let him help her stand as they walked out of the tent with their nettles.

CHAPTER 25

What did she mean by "a moment?" Garrett wondered as he sat across a fire from Cress. It was the evening after their visitors had left to go back to the Wilderose Castle. That morning, he and Cress had been swans when Ravenna pulled Cress aside to talk. Garrett had hoped to eavesdrop on their conversation, but Liam jumped in, apparently deciding that this was an opportune time to instruct Garrett..

"Let us know if your or the raiders' situation changes."

"Thanks for telling me, otherwise I would have kept any news to myself," Garrett couldn't help but quip back.

Liam narrowed his eyes. "Look, I'm not any happier to be working with you again than you are, I'm sure, but this is more important than either of us. At least think about Cress's welfare."

"What is *that* supposed to mean? I always take her protection into consideration," Garrett hissed.

Liam held up his hands and stepped back. "I was just making sure you were still serious about her wellbeing. That's all. I'm glad to see you are."

Before Garrett could question what Liam meant, Ravenna and Cress joined them.

"You ready to go?" Ravenna asked Liam as she wrapped her arms around one of his. Liam's smile became soft as he told her he was.

Garrett couldn't help the pang of jealousy that he felt seeing the two of them together. He had never felt any love for Ravenna, even when she had agreed to marry him, but he did think she was exceptional. He was happy that she had found someone worthy of her. But as he quickly snuck a peek at Cress, it became evident to him that he was jealous of how free Ravenna and Liam were to express their love for one another.

Which brought him back to the present, wondering if Cress liked having a "moment," whatever that meant, with him.

"You're awfully quiet," Cress said.

He focused on Cress, who had an inquisitive look on her face. The shirt she was working on lay in her lap.

He shook his head to clear his thoughts. "Sorry, I just have a lot on my mind."

Coward, he hissed inwardly to himself.

She pursed her lips, but didn't say anything. Instead she picked up some more nettles and began to add them to her weaving.

"What did you mean yesterday by 'having a moment?'" he unexpectedly blurted out.

Despite the warm glow of the fire casting its color on her face, Garrett could still see Cress's cheeks turning bright red.

"It was nothing. I was just annoyed with Ravenna," she finally mumbled.

His heart sank. Of course he wasn't so lucky as for her to be interested in him. Besides, he already knew that she thought he was overly ambitious to the point of using others for his own gain; why would she want to share "moments" with someone like that?

CHAPTER 26

Life fell into a routine after a couple of weeks. Cress and Garrett would wake up as humans inside of the tent, only to leave shortly afterwards so they could have room to spread their imminent wings. Once swans, they ate breakfast, flew, or took turns napping so that when they turned human again, they'd be rested enough to focus on weaving their shirts.

Cress still wished that they could work longer on the shirts each night. No matter how hard she tried to fight through the pain of the nettles, she always seemed to hit a point where she could no longer bear it.

Tonight was no different, and she fought the tears of frustration that were welling up.

"Can you help me with the sleeves?" Garrett's voice broke the silence.

She saw that Garrett had finished the body of his shirt and only had to create the two sleeves before attaching them. Her own shirt's sleeves were currently sitting in her lap - she had put them down in an effort not to cry.

"Which part do you need help with exactly?" she asked as she walked over.

He gestured with his hands toward the nettles and the unfinished shirt. "All of it."

She grinned. "Let's start with how to make one and go from there."

She intended to pick up one of the nettle plants, though she dreaded it, when Garrett's hand swooped down and blocked hers. Startled, she looked up to see a soft smile on his face.

"Do you think you could just teach me without touching them yourself?"

Dumbly, she nodded and cleared her suddenly dry throat to say, "If that's what you want," and then proceeded to explain how they would create the sleeves. Ignoring the quick thumping of her heart.

The sleeves would be woven from a wide rectangle so that when the long edges were sewn together, it would form a big enough cylinder for an arm to go through. Once that was completed, they would sew one circular side to the hole on the body of the shirt.

Cress internally winced when she thought about how these shirts would be the ugliest thing she ever made. Even when she was still a beginner learning to sew with her mother, her earliest creations had turned out better than these were destined to.

She tried to console herself with the thought that no matter the quality of the end result, she'd be free from the captivity of swan life. It was only slightly comforting.

Garrett knew that he should focus on what Cress was saying as she explained all of the steps that he needed to take to make the sleeves, but he was too distracted by how her face lit up whenever she talked about her passion. It was much better to see that lovely glow on her features than to witness her trying and failing to swipe discreetly at her tears.

His heart twinged when he remembered how upset she had seemed earlier. From past conversations, he knew that she was frustrated by the pain from the nettles and how much it slowed them down. He also knew that if he said they should take a break for the night, she would become stubborn and keep working until the blisters from the nettles started to bleed.

He had to think of different ways to stop her from working by distracting her with something else. Tonight, he decided, was as good a night as ever for her to teach him how to make sleeves.

"Okay, now you try."

Garrett was jolted from his thoughts to find Cress looking at him expectantly. He gave a sheepish grin.

"You weren't paying attention, were you?" Cress huffed, but he saw her fighting back a smile as amusement danced in her eyes.

"Not really, no."

"I guess it's pretty late and we might as well get a little bit of sleep." She stood up from her spot next to him and strode towards the tent. "Coming?" She turned to look at him confidently.

Garrett got off of his stump and followed her inside.

CHAPTER 27

The next couple of nights, Cress found herself helping Garrett again with his sleeves. Her hands were thankful that she wasn't touching her unfinished shirt as much as Garratt was touching his. However, it still made her nervous how far behind she was falling comparatively.

"Finished!" Garrett's smile stretched wide and his dark blue eyes lit up with boyish excitement. He stood and held up the shirt for Cress to see.

Cress jumped up and wrapped her arms around Garrett's neck. "Congratulations! Now I just need to finish mine and we'll have broken the curse!"

Heat flooded her face when she realized how close she was to Garrett, but before she could step away, Garrett slipped his arms around the small of her back. She raised her eyes and his softened when they met hers.

She gulped, but couldn't seem to move away when he started leaning towards her. A gentle brush of his lips met hers.

"Cress." His voice rumbled and she never heard her name said with so much desire.

"I –" She stumbled over her words. Warmth flooded her body as he kissed her again. He pressed his lips harder, turning the kiss into something desperate. As if his life depended on this one kiss. She felt another kind of warmth than the one that had spread slowly inside of her. The sun's rays were starting to peak over the eastern horizon. She hadn't realized how late they had been working on their shirts.

She pulled back just as the magical bright light wrapped around them. They were swans again and she still hadn't figured out what to say.

Garrett stepped back from her. "I'm sorry."
Again she did not know how to reply. Garrett waddled to the lake and left her behind to dwell on the fact that she just had her first kiss with the last person she had ever expected to share that moment with.

The water rippled around Garrett as he swam away from Cress and that kiss. Although even the steady paddle of his feet couldn't shake the memory.

He groaned. "How could I have been so stupid?" he asked himself out loud. Cress must hate him. Well, he mused, she must hate him now more than she usually did.

His stomach kept twisting into knots, and despite the fact that he hadn't eaten since the night before, nor had he slept, he was too wired to eat or sleep.

Glancing behind him, he saw that he was too far away from the shore to see Cress, so he finally stopped.

"You're not running away from your mate now, are you?"

Fear shivered down his spine as Willow stepped out from behind the trees, her bright red hair shining in the morning rays.

"Go away," he hissed.

"But my dear, you are far more entertaining than the filthy thugs that I have to work with."

"You could always leave them alone," he suggested, giving in to the fact that the witch wasn't going anywhere.

She made a tsking sound. "Not if I want power to control my own country."

Garrett froze. "What do you mean?" "Let's just say I'm not a pawn in this chess game." Willow winked. Garrett opened his beak to respond, but she continued. "Although, one of those pawns seems to be encroaching on your mate over there."

Garrett blinked and Willow had vanished.

"Cress!"

Lifting his wings out, he started to flap them as he picked up speed on the water. As soon as he was in the air, he pointed his body back to camp.

The hunter that they had hid from previously was sneaking up behind Cress, who had her neck wrapped around her body. She was obviously sleeping and completely unaware of the danger she was in.

Beating his wings as fast as he could, he saw the shirts they had made lying close to where she slept. Without hesitation, he dove toward them, startling the hunter to the point where the hunter fell down. He gave an alarmed honk that woke Cress up.

"Garrett!"

He didn't answer. He was too busy attempting to grasp the shirts in his beak without landing. The stinging in his mouth was sign enough that he got them. Quickly, he flew back to where Cress was and dropped down in front of her.

"Put this on now!" He shouted as he tossed her the shirt that he made.

"But I'm not done with yours!" Cress cried as he picked up the one that she made for him.

"Doesn't matter. There's a hunter coming." Garrett wiggled into the shirt and watched as Cress did the same when she realized that he was committed to putting it on, finished or not.

A bright light flashed and Garrett heard another yelp from the hunter. He didn't think as he dashed in the direction of the shout. With his right arm, he pulled out his sword that rested in the scarab that he was wearing when he was first cursed. He pointed it at the hunter's neck.

"Drop your weapons." His voice sounded hard like the steel of his sword. Rage filled him as he watched the pathetic man who dared attempt to hurt his mate put down his bow and quiver of arrows. Slowly the man got up and raised his hands. Garrett was tempted to dispatch the man, but now that the danger had passed, his thoughts cleared. This hunter might have more information that Liam could use.

"Cress, I need you to find some rope and tie this man up," he said without looking away from his prisoner.

When he didn't hear her move, he flicked his eyes away to check if she was alright and human.

Tears were flowing down Cress's face. "Garrett, your arm."

It was at that moment that Garrett felt something different about his left arm. Without lowering his right arm and the sword pointed at the hunter, he stretched out his other arm only to see that it wasn't his arm, but his swan wing.

CHAPTER 28

Cress had missed feeling the sun on her bare skin. Eyes closed, she lifted her face toward the morning light. She let herself bask in the warmth for a second, but then reluctantly opened her eyes so she could make sure that the curse had broken for Garrett as well.

She gasped when she saw him. He said something to her, but she was too fixated on what was in front of her. Not the fact that he was currently pointing a sword at the man who she recognized as the hunter they followed...but his arm. Or lack of arm.

"Garrett, your arm!"

She gaped as he looked down and noticed that he still had a wing instead of an arm.

Hoseenu, please don't let this mean that he's still in danger of losing his life because of me, she fervently prayed.

"We'll deal with this later, right now I need you to get rope."

She made her way to their pile of supplies inside the tent and searched for the rope she remembered seeing when they first unpacked everything. She found it lying under some flint. Her hands trembled as she reached for it. Clenching it tightly, she returned to Garrett and the hunter.

"I need you to tie him up." He smirked, "Just like before, in the tavern." Cress remembered how she and Ravenna had tied up Garrett's blackmailer while he and Liam made sure he would not get away.

What had her life come to that she was now in the habit of tying up villains? she thought as she followed Garrett's orders.

As she finished securing the rope around the man, she noticed that his face was as pale as a ghost. She worried that he would faint.

"Don't worry. We're not going to hurt you." She tried to be convincing.

The man's eyes flickered briefly from Garrett's sword, which was still pointed at his face, to Cress, but then he focused back on the immediate threat to his life.

"What do you want from me?" the man pleaded.

"Your name."

"Information about your employers."

Cress and Garrett spoke at the same time. Garrett frowned at Cress's request for the man's name. He drew close to her and whispered, "Let me do the talking. We need to take him back to the palace so we can figure out a way to trap the raiders."

"I understand that." Cress rolled her eyes. "But can't you see he's too scared to be of any use until after he's calmed down some?"

They both turned to look at the man, who had indeed fainted. It was Garrett's turn to roll his eyes. "Let's just get back to the castle as soon as possible. We can't figure everything out right now anyway."

Cress watched as Garrett pulled out all of their horses' gear to get them ready for the ride back. It was almost too surreal to think that they'd be leaving their lake. This had been their home for months now, and even though the experience was never one that she would have willingly chosen for herself, nor would she want a repeat of turning into a swan every day, it had provided her with good memories.

A thud brought her out of her musings. Garrett was standing by the horses with the saddles on the ground next to them. His brows furrowed as he looked back and forth between them and the animals that he needed to put them on. The feathers on his left wing looked a little ruffled.

Guilt flooded Cress as she realized that there was no way for Garrett to do all of this with only one functioning arm. She should have finished her shirt long before Garrett had. She was, after all, the seamstress between the two of them.

She ran over to help him. Reaching down, she picked up one of the saddles and put it on his horse. He started to protest, but she ignored him as she tightened the cinch.

Once she finished, she waited for Garrett to lead the hunter, who had awakened while she was busy, onto one of the horses. She tied the rope to the saddle so that the man wouldn't be able to get off on his own.

"We'll share a horse," was all Garrett said to Cress. Cress mounted their horse first and waited for Garrett to climb on and sit behind her. Her back was pressed against his chest and she was thankful he couldn't see the blush blooming on her cheeks.

Garrett passed the second horse's reins to Cress. "Can you hold this so I can steer?"

She took them from him and Garrett nudged their horse to move forward. Cress couldn't help looking over at his wing and felt nauseous thinking that it wasn't fair to Garrett. This was her fault and she would do everything in her power to fix it.

CHAPTER 29

The last several hours had been a whirlwind for Cress. As soon as she and Garrett arrived at the Wilderose Castle with their prisoner, guards swarmed around them. Cress lost track of Garrett as Queen Sophia pulled her inside so they could talk in Cress's bedroom. Not long afterward, Tatiana joined them. They wanted to hear Cress's side of how she and Garrett broke the curse.

The last thing Cress remembered before exhaustion caught up with her and her two friends let her go to sleep was someone saying that Liam and Ravenna should be sent word of her return.

As she woke up the next morning, it was too quiet in her room. No sound of Garrett breathing in his sleep across the room from her. She hadn't realized just how comforting his presence alone was until it was gone.

Thankfully, Yetta coming in to get her ready for breakfast distracted her from the unexpected loneliness that had overcome her.

Walking into the breakfast hall, Cress couldn't help the smile that shone on her face at the sight of Garrett at the table. But she quickly hid her giddiness before anyone could see how much she missed being around him...they had only been apart a few hours! From the quirk of Sophia's eyebrow and the small knowing smile from Tatiana, Cress was pretty sure she wasn't hiding anything. Only Garrett seemed not to notice Cress felt her heart sink in her chest when she spied his wing, remembering once again that she still had to do everything in her power to make it right.

Once Cress sat down and started eating, Sophia cleared her throat. "Now that everyone is here, I want to address the remaining problem in the woods. Since you two are no longer swans, we've lost our ability to see the raiders' hiding spot."

"I might still be able to see it since the curse doesn't seem to be completely broken for me," Garrett spoke up. Cress cringed at the lack of warmth in his voice. She was in the presence of a soldier on a mission - nothing more.

"Tatiana mentioned that except for your arm, the curse and all that it involved has been broken. Wouldn't the barrier consider you human?" Sophia asked.

Tatiana cleared her throat. "The part of the curse that would take his life has been broken, and he won't turn into a full swan if he's not at the lake, but he's not completely human either."

Cress sagged in her chair. He wasn't going to die if something were to happen to her. She deliberately ignored the part of her that had been worried about his life if she were to "no longer be his mate." There was just too much to unpack there, and she didn't have the energy to think about it right now.

"We should still test this theory out before we make plans that depend on it," Sophia said, then turned to focus on Cress. "In the meantime, we still need to prepare for the ball next month. I'm hoping to use it to ask our allies for assistance stopping the raiders once and for all. That means that we need to make sure that our symbols of unity between Lyra and Wilderose are completely ready by then."

"Now that I'm here, I'll check to see what needs to be done. As well as complete fittings for your dress."

Sophia nodded and went back to relaying everything that needed to happen in the meantime.

Garrett had looked at Cress when she spoke, but when she tried to catch his eye, he turned away without any acknowledgement. It felt like a physical blow to Cress. They had gone through so much together in these last few months, not to mention he took her first kiss. Now that the curse was broken, were they no longer going to at least be friends?

Even though she thought he had changed and was no longer the kind of person to use and discard the people around him, this had proven otherwise. She was not going to accept this. She would try to find a way to remove his swan wing, but after that, she would forget his influence on her life. She would forget the kindness he had shown her as a child and the unexpected kiss. It didn't matter if it felt like her heart was bleeding from the sting of a thousand nettles at the thought of losing him.

CHAPTER 30

Garrett was exhausted. He had been going nonstop. First he secured the hunter with the castle guards so that he could be questioned later. Then he met with Tatiana to make sure that enough of the curse was broken.

"It seems to me that you won't be in any danger of dying," Tatiana told him.

"That's good, but what about my arm?" Garrett raised his wing.

Tatiana frowned. "Did Cress not finish the shirt completely?"

Garrett stiffened. "It wasn't her fault. She needed one more night, but I couldn't think of another way to save her as a swan."

"I understand, but unfortunately that doesn't change the fact that you put it on without the last sleeve. Only Hoseenu knows if there's any way to change it back."

Garrett left their conversation feeling discouraged. If even a fairy godmother couldn't change his wing back into an arm, then he would have to live with it for the rest of his life.

Later that day, he wanted to make sure that Cress was alright. However, Queen Sophia caught him on his way to Cress's room and interrupted that intention.

"Are you ready to talk with your captive?" she asked him, skipping pleasantries.

"Yes, Your Majesty." He bowed, his soldier's training kicking in at the interaction with a monarch.

He followed her to Wilderose's dungeons where the Wilderosian soldiers had brought the man who nearly killed Cress. Queen Sophia's bodyguards tacitly escorted them down the halls. When they reached the prisoner's cell, Garrett saw that the man sat hunched over in a corner.

"State your name," Queen Sophia commanded.

The man scrambled to get up and bow as he said, "William, Your Majesty."

"Explain to me why you were poaching on elven territory."

William shuffled on his feet but remained silent.

Garrett opened his mouth, but without breaking her stern gaze on William, Queen Sophia held out her hand to stop him from speaking.

A long, uncomfortable silence filled the space, and only Queen Sophia seemed unphased.

Eventually, William caved. "I was offered more money to hunt on elven land."

"Enough money to tempt you into ignoring the fact that the elves punish poachers by death?"

William looked down at his feet as if they could provide a better answer than the truth. "It was a lot of gold, Your Majesty."

"Who offered you so much gold that you were willing to risk your life?"

William remained silent, and Garrett couldn't help but admire the fortitude of the Wilderosian queen. He could never imagine Ravenna questioning a prisoner with as much resolve as Queen Sophia.

"You have broken elven law by hunting in their woods, so you must be tried by them. However, I can guarantee your penalty will not be death if you give us more information about your employers."

A dam seemed to break in William: all of a sudden he couldn't keep quiet. "I don't know who these people are! I just know that they needed meat for over a hundred men. They didn't even pay me as much as they said they would! They threatened to turn me in to the elves for killing animals on their land. All I know is that they seemed to be planning something big. Bigger than Wilderose. Please, Your Majesty, spare my life."

His words reminded Garrett of what Willow had implied before he had to rescue Cress from the deadly bow and arrow.

"When you are handed over to the elves, I will do everything in my power to convince them to give you an alternative sentence."

"Thank you, Your Majesty," William groveled.

"Don't thank me yet. There are worse punishments than death."

Queen Sophia abruptly walked away, and Garrett did everything he could to keep up with her.

"Your Majesty, William's mentioning that the raiders' plan of something bigger than Wilderose reminded me that the witch made an appearance at the lake this morning."

Queen Sophia stopped walking and turned to face him. "Go on."

"She said something along the lines of working with this group so she could rule her own country. I wasn't able to get more information from her because I realized that Cress was in danger."

Queen Sophia pursed her lips before she spoke. "Are you sure? Because if that's the case, it seems like we need to convince the rest of the countries that they are in just as much danger as we are."

"I'm positive, Your Majesty."

Garrett watched as all of the stamina drained out of her. She pressed one of her hands to her temple. "We'll address this tomorrow morning at breakfast."

"Yes, Your Majesty." Garrett bowed. He started to turn away so he could finally check on Cress, but Queen Sophia called out to him.

"And, Garrett?"

He turned back.

"Cress is asleep right now. Since your life is no longer tied to hers, you should give her space. You both need clear heads to decide what you both want."

Garrett felt like he had been punched in the stomach. "What do you mean?"

"I saw the way that you both interacted at the lake. But you were thrown together in unusual circumstances.

That can create a false sense of unsubstantial intimacy. If Hoseenu sees fit, giving her space will not be the end."

The back of his neck felt hot and he could feel a blush rising up to his face. He knew that he wanted to be with Cress. He knew it right after their visitors had left the lake, and he needed to know if she felt the same way.

But Queen Sophia was right. *He* might know, but Cress needed to figure this out for herself.

"Yes, Your Majesty."

Satisfied, Queen Sophia left, leaving Garrett standing alone.

CHAPTER 31

A week had passed since the curse had broken. Cress found herself absorbed in work. First she checked in on her team that had been working on bringing her designs to life for the five Wilderosian council members. They had made great progress, but there were just a few details that she needed to do herself.

She was also spending a great deal of time on Sophia's dress. From fitting sessions with Sophia, to working on the adjustments on her own time, it felt like she would never be finished in time for the ball. Already dignitaries and foreign monarchs were starting to arrive two weeks early.

All that work didn't distract her from the distance between Garrett and herself. Whenever the two of them ended up briefly alone between events and meals, he was kind but cool towards her. She wanted to scream every time, but reminded herself that she had decided not to care about how he treated her. She was going to make sure that she found a way to restore his human arm and then she'd let him be.

So what if she deliberately quieted down to listen to updates about how he was doing when Sophia or Tatiana mentioned him? That was no one else's business but her own.

However, there was one day that she did bring him up with Tatiana.

"Tatiana, do you think that maybe making another shirt out of stinging nettles would turn back Garrett's arm?" Cress casually asked.

The two of them were alone in the sitting room portion of Cress's room. Cress was making adjustments to Sophia's dress while Tatiana read a report that Ravenna had sent over, along with a notice that she and Liam would be arriving in Wilderose in a few days.

"I don't know. It's possible. Hoseenu has been awfully quiet about the matter every time I ask him." Tatiana sighed.

It was one of the few times when Cress had seen Tatiana so despondent about something.

"It wouldn't hurt to try though, right?" Cress insisted.

"I'm sure it wouldn't, but unfortunately, we also need him to remain half-winged until after we've dealt with the raiders."

Cress couldn't argue with that, but the fact that Tatiana said it was possible to completely break the curse over Garrett gave Cress hope.

That was how she found herself back at the lake in the Elven Wood. It had almost been too easy for her to sneak away after breakfast and saddle a horse from the stables. Unfortunately, the one person who saw her leave was Garrett.

"What are you doing?" The first real words he had spoken to her all week.

"I needed a break and thought a ride would be refreshing."

It was hard not to sound guilty, but she didn't want him to know what she was doing. She wouldn't tell him her plans until after she had created a new shirt for him.

"You're going alone." It wasn't a question.

"Well, yes. Everyone's busy and I'll probably be gone for most of the day and don't want to take up anyone's time."

"I can escort you," Garrett offered.

Cress's heart twisted in longing. As much as she wanted to be alone with him again, this was the one time where it wouldn't be okay if she did. Why hadn't he offered to spend time with her beforehand?

"I'm sorry, but I just need to be alone right now. I've been so busy that I haven't had time to think."

She nearly took back her words when she saw the brief flash of disappointment on his face that he immediately hid behind a stony countenance, but before she could, he said, "Alright. I'll leave you alone then." He left her standing there.

You're doing this for him, she tried to reassure herself.

She had originally tried looking around the castle grounds for stinging nettles, but of course the weed would never have been tolerated by the royal gardeners.

So here she was, back at the place where she knew they definitely grew.

Even though it had only been a week, it was weird being back at the lake. All of their things had been returned to the castle, so it looked like no one had ever lived here. It almost made her tear up, but she pushed aside her nostalgia to focus on her purpose: gathering enough nettles to make a new shirt for Garrett.

She was thankful that this time around she knew how many she needed to pick, so she could fill up her basket with just enough during this one trip.

Hours passed as her basket slowly filled up with all of the stinging plants that she needed. Her hands had started bleeding a long time ago, because she decided that she couldn't wear gloves. If Tatiana hadn't seen fit to give them gloves the first time around, she figured that it was part of the "gift made from suffering" as an element to breaking the curse.

Right before she had enough nettles to create a new shirt, a sudden noise from behind her startled her. Her heart raced as she slowly turned around, trying to keep her breathing even.

Dread consumed her when she discovered what it was, or rather *who* it was. Willow leaned against a nearby tree watching Cress. As soon as Cress made eye contact, Willow spoke. "Imagine my surprise to discover a lack of swans on this lake."

All of Cress's instincts told her to run, but she stood frozen in place. All of Cress's instincts told her to run, but she stood frozen in place, paralyzed by fear. The shaking in her legs told her that at least it was terror and not an enchantment that entrapped her

"Where is our handsome soldier? Or are you out here all by yourself?"

Cress watched helplessly as Willow stood up and walked towards her. She needed to get away, but she had tied her horse to a tree closer to the lake than to the patch of nettles she had been gathering.

"You just missed him," Cress bluffed. "He's scoping out your friends' location."

Willow scowled. "Then I guess we'd better wait for him to get back."

Cress had been hoping Willow would want to ensure that her companions were still safely hidden, but she either didn't believe Cress or didn't care what happened to the raiders. Cress wasn't sure which one she hoped was the reason, but regardless, she needed to get out of there quickly.

Cress scooped up her basket and dashed through the nettle patch and into the trees behind it. Her legs stung from where they brushed past the stinging nettles, but she kept running. The pain was a familiar one and she knew she could fight past it and press on ahead.

Cress could hear Willow shouting after her, but she didn't stop. Deeper and deeper into the woods she ran. For a brief moment it felt like the air around her crackled with lightning, but still she continued to run, clutching her basket to her chest.

It wasn't until the trees started to look like buildings instead of ordinary plants that she realized how far into the Elven Wood she had run. Hope filled her thoughts as she realized that maybe the elves could protect her from the witch's pursuit.

"Help! Somebody help me!" she cried.

No one answered her. When she made it into the middle of a cluster of elvish buildings, she discovered why: the whole area was deserted.

Her chest tightened and she couldn't breathe. Where were the elves? Was this why she and Garrett hadn't seen any during their whole time spent on the lake? They weren't even living in the inner part of their own woods.

She continued straight until she realized that she was in an alleyway leading to a dead end.

"It seems like you've finally discovered that there's no one here to help you."

Spinning around, Cress's heart sank as she saw Willow not far behind her.

CHAPTER 32

Garrett was worried about Cress. She hadn't returned from her ride yet and it was past lunchtime. He had noticed that she hadn't packed a lunch, let alone any other supplies, so he had assumed that she would be back by now.

He couldn't focus on the meeting he was in. Queen Sophia had gathered her advisors, along with Tatiana and himself, to talk about strategies to eradicate the raiders from the Elven Wood now that they knew that he could lead them past the barrier. He felt like everyone was going back and forth, suggesting the same approaches in different ways over and over again. He needed to find Cress. Something was wrong.

"Garrett, where are you going?" Queen Sophia asked him when he stood to leave.

"Cress hasn't returned from her ride. I'm going to go fi nd her." He left without waiting for a reply.

He hadn't made it far from the room when Tatiana caught up with him.

"Do you know where to look for her?" she asked.

Garrett's shoulders dropped and he stopped walking. "No."

Tatiana reached out and placed a hand on his shoulder. She smiled gently. "She asked about nettles recently. It's possible she went to go find some."

"Why would she do that?" Garrett frowned.

Tatiana gave a pointed look at his wing. His eyes widened.

"No. She didn't. Would that even work?"

"I don't know. And I told her as much when she brought it up."

"Doesn't she know that area is dangerous?" he roared. "We were lucky that the hunter found us before the raiders did."

Garrett ran, leaving Tatiana behind. How could Cress put herself in danger like this? What was she thinking?

Please, Hoseenu. Keep her safe! Let me find her unharmed, he prayed as he saddled his horse. He hoped he was anxious over nothing, but he wouldn't stop worrying until he saw Cress for himself.

"Where are all the elves?" Cress demanded when Willow reached the spot where she stood.

Willow tilted her head like a cat looking at a mouse. Cress tried to suppress her shiver, but the smile Willow gave showed that she wasn't successful at hiding her fear.

"The king couldn't have them around. They would have ruined all of his planning."

"What king? Who's behind this?" Cress raised her chin and held her ground. It was foolish to stand up to a witch that had already cursed her once, but there wasn't anywhere left for her to go. She was already cornered; might as well try to learn what was going on.

"Wouldn't you like to know."

"That is why I asked," Cress huffed.

Willow barked out a laugh. "You're still a feisty one. I like that."

Cress cringed. She hadn't meant to be heard, but it was still true. She would like to know, so she tried asking again. "What's in it for you? You're obviously smart and ambitious. You can't be doing all of this," Cress gestured around to the empty elven city, "for nothing."

"A promise that my kind would be free to do whatever they want without Hoseenu's chapel servants getting in the way. A country of our own with me as the ruler. Do you want to see how I fuel my magic?" Willow abruptly asked.

If Cress was afraid before, she was terrified now. All she knew about how witches gained their magic was that it involved stealing blood from humans. It was one of the reasons why witchcraft was banned in all of the countries, and why it would be terrible for there to be a whole country where they would have free reign.

"Not really. As much as I've enjoyed our game of cat and mouse, I think I should leave now."

"Now that's a shame," Willow tsked. Her voice dripped with false disappointment. "But I think it would be very insightful for you to see how it works."

Cress became aware of the spider tattoo starting to wiggle on Willow's wrist. She nearly gagged as it used its front legs to pull itself off of Willow's skin and crawled into her hand.It was no longer a drawing, but a living creature.

"This won't hurt. Much." Willow maliciously smiled as the spider crept off of her hand and used a web to descend onto the ground.

Cress hadn't noticed that she had subconsciously backed away until she was pressed against the wall in the back of the alley. She looked around, desperately searching for something that could assist her, but found nothing of use.

With the spider only inches away from her, Cress raised her foot and tried stomping on the creeping arachnid. Unfortunately, it just flattened itself back into a drawing while it was under her shoe, and raised up again when she stepped away.

"Nice try, darling, but it's inevitable that you'll be my spider's dinner. It takes more than a mere shoe to kill a witch's spider."

"Fire will work."

Both women turned toward the sound of the voice. If she wasn't keeping close watch on the spider's progress, Cress would have continued staring at Garrett's sudden appearance. She would run and jump into his arms if she could.

"You!" Willow shrieked at the sight of the torch Garrett held in his right hand.

"Yes, me. Cress, step on the spider. Now!" Garrett yelled.

Cress gaped at him, but did as he said. The spider again flattened itself into a drawing, unmoving.

Garrett was making his way towards her, but he still had to get past an angry witch. There was no way for him to defend himself while holding a torch with his one human hand. Willow seemed unable to use magic while her spider was not attached to her, but that didn't mean she was completely helpless. She fought Garrett with a swipe of her sharp nails. All he could do was dodge as best as he could.

Cress weighed her options. Her foot was the only thing keeping the spider at bay, but the fire was the only thing that could truly get rid of it.

Coming to a decision, she leapt forward, putting the spider behind her, and jumped onto Willow's back. Cress seized Willow's long red hair in her hands and pulled as hard as she could, wrapping her legs around Willow's waist.

Willow screamed and tried to shake Cress off of her, but Cress hung on as tight as she could. She couldn't see Garrett anywhere, but then again, she was too busy focusing on not letting go of the witch.

Willow wised up and rammed Cress back into a wall. Cress grunted as Willow kept smashing her into the building's side. Then, all of a sudden, Willow started writhing underneath her. It wasn't until Willow's body started to smoke as if it were on fire that Cress hopped off of her. Cress turned to see a small body burning at

Garrett's feet and realized that he had successfully set the spider on fire. Causing Willow to burn as well.

Cress quickly ran over to him. "Garrett!" she cried as she threw her arms around him, and buried her face into his chest as he held her close. The feathers on his wing were soft against the skin showing through the back of her dress where it had torn on the walls. She closed her eyes as if that would help tune out Willow's wails of agony, but it was no use.

It wasn't until there was silence that she finally pulled back from Garrett. She looked up into his face.

"Is she...dead?" she whispered.

Garrett nodded and she sagged in relief. It was over.

CHAPTER 33

Garrett ignored the ashes that were once Willow. He was too busy looking over Cress to make sure she hadn't been seriously injured. He would never forget the moment when he saw the witch's spider heading towards Cress to feast on her lifeblood. He shuddered at the thought of what would have happened if he hadn't found her in time.

"How did you know where I was?" Cress asked him.

"You made it too easy to track you from the lake. All of my fine soldiers' training was wasted." He smirked, but then winced as Cress punched his right shoulder.

"You and your wasted training." She glared at him. However, her gaze softened as she leaned in to hug him. "Thank you for saving me."

"I would say anytime, but I'd rather you not be in situations where you need saving." He chuckled. "But what do you think you were doing out here when you knew the raiders were nearby and Willow was sure to be around?"

Cress wouldn't meet his stare. "I thought that maybe you would feel better if I could fix your arm."

Garrett gaped at her. "What do you mean 'feel better?'"

She rolled her eyes. "You've been acting strange ever since the curse broke, so I figured it must be because you were mad that I hadn't finished your shirt before we put them on."

"Cress, look at me." He waited until she did. "I wasn't mad. I knew that you weren't finished, but you were in danger as a swan. I couldn't let anything happen to you, so I had us put the shirts on. If anyone is to blame for my arm being a wing, it's me."

"But –"

He cut her off. "And besides that, I've been acting 'strange', as you put it, because I thought you would need space from me." Now he was the one who couldn't meet her gaze. "I love you, but I didn't want our experience as swans to the only thing keeping us together together. It seemed like a good idea to give you time on your own to decide what you wanted."

"You love me?" Cress whispered.

Garrett looked back at her and saw tears well up in her eyes. He started to panic. "I do, but I know how you feel about me and I promise not to act – "

"I love you." This time Cress interrupted him.

"Yep." She said with an emphasis on the 'p'. Despite how casual she tried to say it, Garrett watched as a soft smile filled her face. He could hardly believe this was happening to him.

With a soft smile of his own, he cradled her face

with his hand, and leaned down to kiss her. It wasn't like the first time when he just barely grazed his lips on hers. He made sure that he put all of his love for her into this one. There was a moment of hesitation on her part, but then he felt her starting to kiss him back. It was a kiss filled with longing and the need to express their love for each other.

Garrett was reluctant to end it, but they needed to return to the castle. It still wasn't safe out here, especially now that they knew for sure that the elves were missing.

"What are you doing?" Cress pouted.

"We need to head back."

"Fine, but we better pick up where we left off ."

"Of course," Garrett chuckled.

Cress couldn't believe everything that had happened. First, she and Garrett killed a witch. The next thing she knew, he was telling her that he loved her. Now they were back in Sophia's office in the Wilderose Castle telling Sophia and Tatiana everything about the missing elves and what Willow had said, conveniently skipping over the part about the kisss afterwards.

"What do you mean the elf city is deserted?"

Cress was shocked to see tears in Sophia's eyes when she asked them for more details.

"It's like we said. No one was around, and Willow had implied that it was part of some plan that some king is behind." Garrett repeated.

"Do you think she meant a current king, or someone calling himself king?" Tatiana asked.

Cress shrugged, "It wasn't all that clear."

"It must be someone with a lot of influence," Garrett added. "Otherwise, he wouldn't have been able to gain so many followers."

"That's true. We might have an enemy in our midst at the ball in a couple of weeks." Sophia mused. She still looked shaken up, and Cress wished that it were just the two of them so she could ask her what was wrong.

"Thank you for letting us know, and I'm so sorry that all of this has been your experience of Wilderose. Cress, I would completely understand if you wish to return home to Lyra," Sophia said. "Although, Garrett, I hope that you will stay to help us in the upcoming fight with the raiders since you really are the only one that can lead us to their hideout."

"I'm not going anywhere," Cress interjected after Garrett bowed his head. "There's a ball coming up, and I need to make sure all of your outfits are perfect. Besides, Ravenna and Liam are arriving soon, so everyone I love will all officially be here. I can't leave you alone with someone plotting to take over." She crossed her arms over her chest and dared anyone to tell her otherwise.

Sophia let out a laugh, but it sounded closer to a sob. "Thank you, Cress. Now if you'll excuse me."

Everyone watched as Sophia hurried away through the door in the direction of her suite. Tatiana, Garrett, and Cress wordlessly left through the other door toward the main portion of the castle.

"I'm so thankful that Hoseenu protected you both today," Tatiana said. She reached over and hugged first Garrett and then Cress. "I've been so worried for both of you." She walked away, leaving Cress and Garrett alone in the hallway.

"It's not too late for you to return to Lyra," Garrett said.

Cress huffed, "Nice try, but you're stuck with me."

Garrett reached out with his right arm, wrapping it around her shoulders and squeezing her close to his side. "I wouldn't have it any other way."

He leaned down and kissed her. Cress agreed. She, too, wouldn't have it any other way.

EPILOGUE

"Ravenna! I need you to stop moving!" Cress looked up in exasperation from her kneeling position on the floor. They were in Ravenna's and Liam's guest suite in the Wilderose Castle. Cress had been excited to see her best friend and wanted to fill her in on everything that had happened. It had been great to catch up with her...until Ravenna pulled out the dress that she was planning on wearing to the ball.

Cress could not in good conscience let the queen of Lyra wear something as unflattering as the formless blue dress that Cress thought she had disposed of the last time she went through Ravenna's closet.

Without the time needed to create a whole new dress, Cress decided that she would cinch up the current dress so that it could show off Ravenna's curves and allow the skirt to flare out.

The only problem was that Ravenna was the worst model during fittings,always fidgeting as if she would die if she were to cease moving. Cress thought it was Ravenna's only true flaw.

A knocking sound at the door came right before it opened up to reveal Sophia. "May I come in?"

"Of course you may!" both Ravenna and Cress exclaimed.

Sophia sat at one of the nearby settees and watched as Cress continued working on adjustments and tried, but failed, to not poke Ravenna with a needle.

"Did Liam or Garrett find out anything about where the elves could be located?" Ravenna asked.

Sophia leaned forward to rest her head in her hands. "No, and I'm so worried. How could a whole magical race disappear like this?"

Cress saw the necklace Sophia always hid under her bodice dangling out. The stargazer lily pendant was beautiful, and even from a distance Cress could tell that it was made by an elf. She also knew that the necklace had to have been made by someone who had known Sophia well enough to know her favorite flower.

"We'll figure this out. I promise," Cress tried to reassure her friend.

"It's just another piece of the mystery that we're already trying to solve. We're now a lot closer to learning about what's going on than we were a year ago." Ravenna added.

Sophia looked up and gave a wan smile. "Thank you. Both of you."

Hoseenu, help me to keep that promise, Cress prayed.

THE SLEEPING QUEEN

THE LYRIAN ALLIANCE

BOOK THREE

Coming fall 2023

ACKNOWLEDGEMENTS

Behind every book there are so many people who made it come to life.

In no special order of importance:

Thank you to everyone at Enchanted Ink Publishing. Seriously. You've had to put up a lot with my constant missed deadlines. I owe Meredith, Natalia, and Greg so much chocolate/tea/coffee/all the good things they love, because The Swan Wing is only here, because they were the ones who unknowingly kept me going.

Again, thank you to those that worked at Damonza.com for The Swan Wing's cover! It's the first thing

Thank you Lauren for all of your feedback and making this even better.

Thank you to Amber for all of your copy edits. Especially after having a baby this year!

To all of my friends and family, thank you for always checking in on the second book to get me into gear.

Everyone who read The Cursed Queen and got excited for book two. Especially the students at the school where I'm a librarian. Seeing your excitement about wanting to read The Swan Wing makes my day.

I want to thank God for giving me the grace to write this book and see it to the end!

ABOUT THE AUTHOR

COLLEEN FORBES is an author based in the greater Seattle area where she loves to write fairy tale retellings.

After becoming a computer programmer, she tried out a few different roles before writing her first book, The Cursed Queen. In addition to writing, she is also a librarian, dog enthusiast, and a follower of Jesus.

When not reading in her home library hidden behind a secret bookshelf door, you can find her having adventures with her Black Labrador Retriever, Lila.

www.ingramcontent.com/pod-product-compliance
Lightning Source LLC
Chambersburg PA
CBHW030520310726
48979CB00010B/1748/J

* 9 7 8 1 9 5 3 5 6 8 0 3 8 *